Triple Crown Publications presents . . .

Cream

A compilation by

Tu-Shonda Whitaker
*

Dan___ _antiago

Compilation and Introduction copyright © 2004 by
Triple Crown Publications
2959 Stelzer Rd., Suite C
Columbus, Ohio 43219
www.TripleCrownPublications.com

Library of Congress Control Number: 2005930553
ISBN# 0-9767894-1-8
Cover Design/Graphics: www.MarionDesigns.com
Editor: www.PhoenixBlue.com, Maxine Thompson
Junior Editor: Sheniqua Sharp
Editor-In-Chief: Mia McPherson
Consulting: Vickie M. Stringer

First Trade Paperback Edition Printing
10 9 8 7 6 5 4 3 2

Printed in the United States of America

Cream

TW

The Last Run

Triple Crown Publications presents . . .

<u>Acknowledgements</u>

God is good all the time...and all the time God is good. May His praise forever be in my mouth, as it is only through His grace and mercy that I've been Blessed.

To my mother who reads everything that I write a hundred times over, to my father who always says, "Shonda, where do you come up with this stuff?" to my daughters: Taylor and Sydney who keep me on my toes and to my husband who never complains about me being on the computer at 5 a.m. – I could never say thank you enough. Your love and support are as much a part of my writing career as my imagination is.

To my grandmother, aunts, uncles, cousins, in-laws, SWAP and sistah-girlfriends, I love every one of you and thank you for your constant love and support.

To my cousin John Whitaker, I don't have to say the reason why I'm so proud of you, because I know you know why. And no, Kaareem I didn't forget you. I'm proud of you too. You and John are like the big brothers I've never had.

Danielle Santiago, gurl where do we begin? First of all let's start by saying that you are wearing the hell outta that crown (smile). You are not only a friend who is always ready to defend or a sister that I can talk with for hours on end, but you are also a woman who has the world in her back pocket. So, I hope you don't mind that I tell everyone I see buying your book, "Oh that's my friend and I have an autographed copy."

Keisha Ervin, you have it all, the beauty, the wisdom, and the talent. Now all you have to do is take the world by storm! And by the way I can still hear Kyrese telling you, "Keisha, get up and come fix me something to eat." (Ha-Ha).

Nakea Murray, you know you my gurl right? Trust and believe nobody can share a bond with Lyfe the way we do. There is no denying that you are a great publicist but more than that you are a greater friend! And by the way I beat you to the O.P.P. ring tone, Ma.

Vickie Stringer, thanks for always being on the other end of the phone when I needed to chat, needed words of wisdom or to just kick it for a few. And guess what? Now every time I hear Cassidy rapping, " ...Better ask about me..." I think of you. Stay real, stay true, and always be Blessed sistah gurl.

Lisa Gibson-Wilson I will keep the words simple but the meaning is abundant, always treat yourself to the best and never let anyone tell you, convince you or show you otherwise.

Melody Guy, I'm happy to be working with you.

K'wan, what an honor it is to have been in the presence of the ole great and gangsta one. K. Elliot, as always it's been a pleasure! Fetish is the bomb baby! Hey Sakinah and Nicole (can't wait for you to read this one) Hey Tamela Fletcher! Hey Pashin! Hey Dawn! Creative Impressions, Source Of Knowledge and Brandon McCalla thanks for your support. Treasure E. Blue, you know, Lil' Love and I got you, Boo! Selena James, how wonderful it has been. You are a marvelous person and I have had such fun meeting and working with you.

To all of my co-workers, your support has been endless and I thank you for that. To my unit members— we're down like four flats ya'll (smile). I want you to know that you are all beautiful and you have an outstanding leadership quality, what we do is not easy but at the end of the day the reward of making the difference in a child's life makes it all worth it!

Mia, Tammy and the entire TCP staff, let's make it happen baby! Thanks for all of your hard work.

Saving the best for last, to the fans, I love each and every one of you. Thanks for the emails and believe me I read them all and can't wait to hear from you on this one. Email me at info@tushonda.com.

Now, are you ready for another hit? Well then, turn the page and let's do the damn thing!

One Love and many Blessings

Tu-Shonda

The Last Run

Part 9: Re-Up

"TRUE STORY," Sef exhaled into a cloud of smoke, while passing the blunt, "A nigga glad you home B."

Bruh cracked a sly smile and eased the blunt into the side of his mouth. He sat on the bottom step of his front porch, leaning on one elbow. His legs were gapped open and the waist of his baggy jeans slid down, just enough to reveal the waistband of his white CK boxers. His wife beater clung to his chest and the tongue of his Tims flapped slightly over the untied laces. Bruh sat silently, watching the street, and nodding his head to an internal beat.

"Sup?" Sef continued, "Speak. You home nigga, on the real, tell me how that shit feel."

"On the real," Bruh removed the blunt from his lips and held it between his fingers like a cigarette,

"I can still feel them tight ass handcuffs connect-
ed to them stiff ass shackles and shit." Bruh took
a drag, "And yo, every time it's real quiet all I can
hear is metal gates slammin' and niggas yellin'
'get off the phone' and *'suck my dick, ya' punk bitch!'*"
Bruh closed his eyes, took another drag, and
passed the blunt back. "Now on the real, *that's*
how a nigga feel."

Sef took a drag, "Come on man, don't fuck up
my high."

"You asked, shit. As far as I'm concerned I
might be home but all this out here," Bruh pointed toward the street, "ain't nothin' but an extend-
ed prison yard. Especially since I'm back to run-
nin' the game, I'm like a fresh nigga in a new
prison . . it's only a matter of time before I meet an
unexpected shank."

"Yo, don't even speak that B."

"Nigga please. You better learn how to keep the
eyes in the back of ya neck focused; and look
behind your back 'fore a nigga tryna dick you in
the ass." Bruh looked at his watch, it read nine
o'clock. "Ai'ight," he yarned, "I'll get up."

"Ai'ight yo." Sef gave Bruh a pound. "Be easy."
Sef walked off the porch and Bruh walked up the
stairs. For a spilt second Bruh stood at the front
door, waiting to hear the warning buzz, for the
door to slide back. As the cool summer breeze blew
across his face, he realized what he was doing.

"Shit," he chuckled, "I almost forgot." Bruh took his house keys out of his back pocket and opened the door. He'd been sitting on the porch with Sef for over an hour and this was the first time he was entering his house, since being released from prison this morning.

Bruh was amazed to see that in two years not much had changed. His shit was still hooked - black leather living room set with black and white suede pillows, oriental rug, with an operating aquarium as the coffee table. On the wall, opposite the couch, were a 42-inch plasma TV and a paper-thin CD player, both hooked up to the surround sound and the speakers in the ceiling.

Bruh walked around the house, checking things out. He couldn't believe that none of his daughter's toys were strolled about. The last he remembered, Tomika never cleaned up. "Humph." He looked around, "This is proof that the broad is never home. Now I know fa' sho' she be gettin' her killer pussy on."

This is some bullshit Bruh thought as he continued to roam about. The soles of his Tims slapped against the wooden floor, causing him to involuntarily peek around every corner. He tried not to but he couldn't help it; like a nervous twitch it was something that he couldn't fight. After all, it was how he survived the last two years in prison.For Bruh, prison had been more than a place. It was a culture, attached to a forced religion that only an exorcism could bring him out of.

Now in his bedroom, Bruh placed his Tims side by side, in a neat row, next to his king size sleigh bed. He removed the bag of weed tucked in his back jeans' pocket and placed it on the night-stand, before proceeding to fold his jeans. He took off his white wife beater and folded it as well. Then he placed it on top of his jeans and laid the folded clothes on the chaise lounge. *Damn nigga,* Bruh looked around, *Yo' ass is home now, you don't have to go to bed 'cuz it's nine o'clock. It ain't lights out no more. Turn on the TV, the radio, call Tomika, or something."*

Bruh picked up the phone and dialed Tomika's cell, but there was no answer. *"This bitch,"* he huffed, hanging up. He picked up the universal remote and turned on the radio and plasma TV simultaneously. At least for tonight, he needed as much noise as he could find. The house was too quiet and he needed something to let him know he was still alive.

"I can't take this shit." Bruh took the bag of weed and started packing another blunt. "I should'a just stayed in the street with Sef, at least for tonight. This just don't feel right. I swear, I'm fucked up. Two year bid and home feel like it done moved. What kinda shit is this?"Bruh lit the blunt and took a drag.

"Yo," he laughed, blowing out the smoke, "I

swear, nigga, this is it. You got one more road to cross and one more risk to take. After this you're done. You gon' make this last run, beat that street, make that money, get you a square, then we out— Agreed? A-mother-fuckin'- greed."

Bruh finished the blunt and mashed the remains into the ashtray. As the high of the weed began to take a nice effect, he laid back on the bed. The D.J., Sherry Martinez, was on the radio handling 105.1's night show. Her choppy Puerto Rican accent was sexy to his ears and the sweetness of her words trickled down his spine. Bruh closed his eyes, massaged his ten-inch dick, trapped his own vision of Sherry Martinez underneath his heavy eyelids, and peacefully drifted into another world.

* * * *

Beads of sweat oozed from his temples like an internal thunderstorm. He tossed and turned with his back resting against the bed and his feet planted on the floor. The alarm clock had started its daily 6 a.m. sizzle, which seemed to travel through the air and grab a hold of Bruh's skin. He began to toss wildly in his sleep. The sizzle created a harsh buzzing sound that was invasive and designed to scare its listeners awake. As the sizzling chant of the alarm clock seeped deeper into his ears, Bruh whispered in a low tone, *"Shake down . . . shake down . . . shake down . . . shake down . . . shake down."* As the sizzle became louder so did

Bruh's ranting and when the alarm reached it's highest peak and went soaring into the air, Bruh jumped up. With beads of sweat drenching his body, he screamed, *"Oh shit, Rob, wake up! It's a shake down!"*

Bruh jumped off the bed, *"701652 at attention."* As he spat out his prison number he braced himself for the battering of the C.O's in riot gear. Still not conscious of his surroundings, Bruh started to call his old cellmate's name. *"Rob! Yo Rob! Say yo' ma'fuckin' number, nigga! You got cancer man. You like a father I never had, please say that ma'fuckin' number! You not gon' survive no more time in the hole."* When Bruh didn't hear a response from Rob, he felt like he wanted to cry. Rob was all he had in prison, the only man in his life that ever made him feel like something. *"Shit,"* Bruh thought, *"Rob's shank."* Bruh spun around and lifted up his mattress and found . . . not a ma'fuckin thing but two twin box springs.

"Oh shit!" Bruh shook himself awake. Thick beads of blinding sweat slid into his eyes as he desperately tried to remember where he was. He wiped the sweat and his blurry vision became clear. He looked around the room in a fast forward motion. He focused on the furniture, looked down at the floor, and then turned to see the plasma TV mounted on the wall.

He took a deep breath and as he exhaled he felt a warm trickle running down his leg. When he looked, the entire front part of his boxers was covered in fresh piss. "Damn, Bruh," he said to himself. "First night home and you pissin' on ya'self. That's some shit."

Bruh went to the bathroom, grabbed a bar of soap and prepared to take a shower. Turning on the mix of hot and cold water, he heard soft footsteps creep up behind him. Delayed in his reaction to attack, his sudden fear forced him to drop the soap, as he felt his dick being palmed and gently pulled.

"You know the routine nigga," whispered a raspy female voice, "You ain't never s'pose to drop the soap!"

Bruh chuckled in disbelief, *This bitch just don't get it.* From the sound of the voice and the soft pull on his dick, he knew the person was Tomika, his daughter's mother. Instead of turning around, he removed her hand, picked up the soap, and stepped into the shower.

Immediately he began to lather up. Ignoring the hint, Tomika quickly undressed, and stepped in behind him. She started massaging Bruh's ass with one of her cold hands while taking the other and gently pulling the skin back and forth on his uncircumcised dick. His body stiffened. He turned around and finally greeted her.

Bruh looked at her naked body and saw that nothing had changed. It was still a bangin' size eight, tight to the frame, and dipped in mocha. The steamy water beaded on her rich skin sparkled like wet diamonds. He swallowed hard when he remembered how she used to make him come. *This bitch can suck a dick,* he thought to himself, looking at Tomika drop to her knees. Streams of the steamy water splashed back and forth over her bouncing head, while she licked the length of his erotic friend.

"Don't pull out, I'ma swallow." Grabbing the base of his dick Tomika circled her tongue around the head, while playing with the precome oozing in her mouth. Bruh, took a deep breath and lifted her head up. "Where you been? And where's my daughter?"

Tomika responded by swallowing his dick whole. This was making the situation of getting rid of her difficult. Bruh slowly slid his wet dick from between her full lips. "I asked you a question."

"The question *is,* what are *you* doing here?" Tomika snapped. "And Milan's with my grandmother."

"She better be with your grandmother. And what am *I* doing here? This is *my* house, Ma."

"That's true, Boo, but I live here with you," Tomika said as she got off her knees.

"For now." Bruh sucked his teeth. He squinted his eyes and thought about his last conversation with Rob and then with Sef on the ride home from prison. "That bitch is cut," he'd said.

"Why?" Rob and Sef both asked.

"'Cuz she ain't shit. The last time she came to visit me, she smelled like Obsession for men. I smacked the shit outta her in the visiting hall and told her not to ever come the fuck back!"

Standing in the shower, with water splashing all over their bodies, Bruh wanted to do Tomika, badly, but he was trying his best, not to take it there. Tomika wasn't the type that a nigga's dick could just run through, there was somethin' about fuckin' her that brought out her stalker streak.

"Come on Bruh," Tomika sucked his right nipple with his dick in her hand, "You know you want some."

He gently pushed her away from him and continued to stare at her. His eyes darted from her hard violet nipples to her ebony-laced-short-and-curly-haired pussy.

Bruh took a deep breath; his dick was ready to bust. He picked Tomika up and she wrapped her legs around his waist. The shower shot jet streams down his back and over his tight ass. He worked his hard dick inside her as far as he could, grinding the swollen head into her expanding wall . . . pushing deeper . . . and deeper . . . and deeper . . . until her pussy jaws clamped shut and all that was exposed to the elements of the warm shower were his balls, slapping against her ass, as she pounded up and down.

Tomika wrapped her legs tighter around Bruh's waist. With her back against the wall, she continued to grind as if she were tilling fresh soil. Bruh stood there waiting for his blood to come to a boil so that he could bust a good nut, and be ghost.

Two minutes later the nut broke loose, which was a minute longer than what he'd planned. Tomika sucked her teeth, "What was that? You ain't never fucked me and came in less than a second."

"First of all, it was two minutes." He pointed to the shower clock, "And another thing, you know you ain't got it like that, so stop pretending."

"Pretending? Bruh, I been here, taking care of this house and our daughter."

"Stop the lies." Bruh cleaned his dick. "You ain't been doin' shit but being a jump off and fuckin' dirty niggas on my bid. Passin' my daughter off to your lil' skeezin' ass, broke-the-fuck-up girlfriends." He stepped out of the shower and wrapped a towel around his waist.

"Whatever!" Tomika huffed, as she dried off. "Don't hate! Shit, didn't you need a trade? Why don't you tell me how to press numbers into a license plate, you G.E.D. needin' ma-fucker. Steppin' to me all sideways and shit." Tomika waved her hand, "Pssst, you 'on't know? You better ask about me?"

"Ask about you? Well who the fuck am I suppose to ask? You better get you some glasses, you cock eyed bitch, so you can see who you talkin' to, fo' I smack the shit outta you! Fuck around and get your lung collapsed, tryna be down. Now look, you can make this easy or you can make it hard. I wanna set you up in a lil' spot, buy you a ride, and give you some cash, so it ain't that bad on your own. But we can't stay in the same house and since this is my shit, you gotta go."

"Set me up in my own spot?" Tomika frowned. "Buy me a ride? You standing here putting me out, and you think I should believe that shit?!" She stepped out of the bathroom and into the bedroom, knocking over anything in her path.

"Tomika!" Bruh said sternly, as he followed her. "Don't get ya neck broke, breaking up my shit."

"Nigga, you just came home from jail and you shittin' on me? You better go check them chickens you got in the street!" Tomika grabbed a pair of jeans and a pink baby doll tee out the closet.

"What the fuck is that suppose to mean?" Bruh twisted his face.

"Oh now you wanna hear from me? Fuck you!" Tomika threw her hands in his face, "So what you sayin' Bruh, you ain't feeling me? After you just fucked me!"

"Aww shit, see I knew fuckin' you would bring

out the stalker in yo' ass. Don't start followin' me."

"Kiss my ass!"

"Yo," he chuckled in disbelief, "Whatever."

"So you really ain't feelin' me?" Tomika placed her hand on her hip.

Bruh stood still and let his silence answer the question.

"Fuck you!" she screamed, "You think somebody should be sweatin' yo' crazy lookin' ass! Nigga, please." She mushed him with all her might in the center of his forehead.

Bruh grabbed Tomika's right wrist and squeezed tightly in on the two bones, "Don't put your hands on me." He took a deep breath. "I'm trying not to break ya face open! *I said* I'm not feelin' yo' ass. Trust me, I ain't fuckin' beat. Now I'm tryin' not to play you, but you'll a make a nigga pimp yo' retarded ass, and have you on the stroll lookin' for ya'self."

"Spare me." Tomika snatched her wrist from Bruh's grip. "You better stop tryna be large and remember you just a local ass nigga. Get the fuck offa me and start flippin' on them fake ass Junior Mafia ma'fuckers you got throwin' bricks fo' yo' ass, fo' you be sent back to jail on some mo' bullshit!"

Beads of water that hadn't dried yet, ran down

Bruh's shoulders like heavy rain sliding down a windshield. He'd gained at least twenty pounds of sheer muscle since he was in prison and now weighed 225 pounds. The prison's weight room had been graceful to a nigga's temple. Not only did Bruh stand six-and-a-half-feet tall, now he had mountains of muscles tumbling down his honey glazed arms and chest like hard waves in the ocean. His pecs seemed to glow as if the sun were rising on them.His thighs were thick, tight, hard, and flawlessly covered with golden choco-late.

Bruh walked up so close to Tomika that she practically had no room to breathe. He grabbed her around the neck and applied just enough pressure to the veins on the side to let her know that if he squeezed any harder, he could kill her. "What you say, bitch? You tryna say somebody set me up? What you tryna say?Repeat it!"

"Get the fuck off me!" Tomika coughed, trying to· wiggle herself free. When she realized that Bruh's grip was too tight to easily get out of, she started to gag. "Let . . . me . . . go." Tomika managed to spit out.

Bruh pushed her slightly as he released his grip on her neck. "You got a month to get the fuck out!"

"A month?" Tomika coughed again, trying to catch her breath. "You just gon' put your child and me in the street? You a sorry nigga! A fuckin' prison yard deadbeat. You the bitch!"

"Please, beat it with that bullshit. Yo' ass was just a fertile ass nut that hung around too long. Now check it, my daughter ain't never got to worry about being in the street, cause I'ma take care of her. I tried to give you the same option, but you standing here trying to play me and shit. But I tell you what," Bruh turned and pulled open the nightstand's drawer to check for his .22, Ruger .9mm, cell phone, and keys to his Hummer. "You let me find out that you know about somebody settin' me up, and you and that nigga are both done!" He paused, "As a matter of fact, I changed my mind. You got *two weeks* to get the fuck out!"

"Boy, please!" Tomika chuckled, even though she knew this wasn't a joke. "How you just gon' end things like this? We got a baby together; I live with you."

"I ain't lived with you in two fuckin' years, so the adjustment of you not being here should be an easy one. Yo' ass is just ungrateful, don't appreciate shit and now you standin' in my face tryin' to fuckin' game me. I should put my knee in your neck for even talking slick!"

"I wasn't talking slick. I been down fo' you nigga. I kept both yo' cell phones on, your gun loaded and everything."

"Bitch, please. You sound ridiculous! All you

about is gettin' money. You ain't holding shit down but your fuckin' feet to the ground. I'm the one who was in prison and still managed to maintain my hustle, kept my blocks straight, and sent niggas with money for you while I was gone. And what you do? Buy clothes and fuck dirty niggas! Now bounce!"

Tomika looked at Bruh as if he'd lost his mind. She waved her hand, slipped on her clothes, and ran down the stairs, slamming the door behind her.

Bruh smirked and proceeded to get dressed. He put on a pair of baggy Army fatigues, a tight, crisp white-wife beater that showed off his seven tattoos: his mother's name in script with R.I.P. next to it, was on the side of his neck. On his left arm was a black panther with green eyes, a lion in full roar, and his daughter's name in block letters running from his forearm into his hand. On his right arm was a cross, an ankh, and the complete verse of Psalm 23. Each tattoo curved seductively over his protruding muscles.

He slipped on a green baseball cap and reinforced the curve in the brim, until it was bent like a half moon over his gray eyes.

Before leaving out the house, Bruh tucked his .22 on the right side of his loosely tied Tim and placed the Ruger at his waist. He grabbed the keys to his Hummer and walked out the front door.

Bruh's intentions were to pick up Sef, make his appearance known throughout his blocks, then get his daughter from Tomika's grandmother and spend the rest of the evening getting to know her. Milan was four years old now, and he was sure that when he saw her, it would be like meeting her again for the first time. Just the thought of spending uninterrupted time with her made him smile.

Bruh slid into his black Hummer. He hadn't sat in his truck in two years and the softness of his custom-made leather seats felt like butter. He put in a classic Biggie CD, "Life After Death," adjusted the side mirrors and relaxed his seat. He sat back with a slight lean to the side, gripped the steering wheel with one hand, and took off.

Riding slowly down the blocks that he loved dearly, Bruh checked out all of the sights, the street signs, and the new additions to the neighborhood. The mid-June heat was sweltering and Bruh loved every bit of it. The sun reflected off the mirror and blinded him a little, but he played it cool. The Hummer's windows were all the way down and the high-pitched sounds of the Newark, New Jersey streets beat themselves into his soul. People that Bruh hadn't seen in two years yelled his name as he whizzed past them.

When he crossed over Bergen Street and Lyons Avenue, he made a U-turn in the middle of the street, going toward Beth Israel Hospital. Once h was where he wanted to be he double-parked his Hummer and watched Zion carry three bags of groceries onto her porch.

Bruh's mind began to drift as he grazed Zion's body with his eyes, thinking about the first time his heart started checking for her. In the beginning they were all close, Bruh, Tomika, and Zion. Zion and Tomika had been girls since high school. So when Bruh got with Tomika, it seemed natural that they all clicked. Being as close as they were, it was nothing for Zion to stop by Tomika and Bruh's spot when Tomika wasn't there, or call on the phone to just kick it with Bruh only. Then came the times when Zion needed a ride home, before she got a car . . . and Bruh somehow made his way into her house to use the bathroom, to use the phone, or to just kick it for a few, which led to late night talks about Bruh and Tomika's problems. Zion would rub his baldhead, hold his hand, and encourage him to do the right thing because if nothing else, he and Tomika had a child together.

But as the universe would have it, that flipped and months later Zion became the one who needed the advice. Bruh broke it down to her exactly how men thought, he taught her the art of real recognizing real and that if she treated a nigga the same way that he treated her, she was sure to get what she wanted.

Eventually the shit came full circle, and Tomika began talking about Bruh to Zion. Tomika complained that Bruh was not showing her love anymore, despite the fact that she was cheating on him. Zion did her best to hold her feelings for Bruh back and instead of professing her own love, she encouraged Tomika to be faithful because Bruh was a good man.

Then came the breakdown, Tomika didn't listen to Zion. "Besides," Tomika figured, "What the fuck does Zion know about a nigga like Bruh?" As far as Tomika was concerned she was the one with the bangin' ass body, down for whatever, and had been wife'n ballers for most of her young adult, twenty-four-year-old, life . . .

Zion was a thick size fourteen. She had a son with a dead beat daddy. Her gear was ai'ight, and yeah, she rocked name brand but she wasn't workin' BeBe, Juicy, Apple Bottom or nothin' like that, not to mention she was square as hell. College degree, average nine-to-five, never been to jail, never did no time for a nigga, only hit a blunt once or twice, and was clearly not ready to ride or die. She was just cool as hell, could offer some wonderful advice, and was there to keep Milan, if need be. Needless to say, Tomika slept on her.

As time went on, Bruh started looking forward to the way Zion smiled, the way she looked at him and blinked her eyes, squeezed his hand, and kissed his baldhead. She encouraged him and although neither one of them wanted to be the first to take it there, they still couldn't control the involuntary stares, the laughs that lasted a few minutes too long, and the occasional brushes against one another. They seemed to have mastered the art of pretend and instead of acting like sexually frustrated wannabe lovers, they carried themselves like the best of friends.

Bruh loved the way Zion would always get up to cook for him at one and two o'clock in the morning. No matter the time, she always answered the door. She never asked him what he was doing to be up so late because she always knew he would say, "Movin' dope Ma. You know the drill." Therefore, she avoided the question and instead acted as if all were well with the world, and that absolutely nothing was strange about her girlfriend's man spending late nights at her house.

This went on for close to a year and then Bruh went to prison without saying goodbye. Bruh was at the last two-year mark of his five-year probation sentence for possession. He was happy to be nearing the end because finally he'd be free and he could get his fat-ass probation officer out of his face. Plus, he was sick of the game; he had bypassed state level and went straight to Fed weight. And yeah the money was sweet, but mo' money equaled mo' problems. Jealous niggas came out of the woodwork, some of them even in Bruh's own camp and he was sick of the constantly on-guard shit. Once his probation was over, he swore to put his constitution into effect, which was, *Express how he felt to Zion and get the fuck out the game.* He'd called Zion earlier that day. "Wassup, Ma. Miss me?" he laughed.

"Boy, please." Zion chuckled, wanting badly to say *yes*"Why, you miss me?"

"Yeah," Bruh said seriously

"Really?" Zion bit the corner of her lip.

"I need to talk to you and lay some shit on the table."

"I'll wait for you."

"Please do."

After he hung up with Zion, Bruh and Sef commenced to packing up close to a million dollars worth of dope. Once they were finished, they moved the work to a rented van, and their driver, Gwen, headed for the monthly D.C. run.

Bruh was so exhausted from stepping on and packing up dope that he fell asleep on the couch. An hour later, the DEA kicked his door in. They threw him to the floor, slapped handcuffs on him, and proceeded to tearing his house apart. When they were done, all they could find was an unregistered Desert Eagle. Pissed that they didn't find the drugs they were looking for, the FEDS snatched Bruh from the floor and threw him in the backseat of their undercover car.

For six months, Bruh was held in county jail,

held without a bail. When he finally went to trial, his lawyer proved that the NARCS never read him his rights or informed him that he was being arrested. The case was dismissed and the prosecutor who was pissed with the technicality, pressed upon the court that Mr. Sean Umar Price, better-known-as, "Bruh," be remanded to custody for violation of his probation. After all, he *was* in the presence of an illegal firearm. The judge agreed and Bruh was sentenced to serving the remaining two years of his probation in prison.

Once he got to prison he couldn't take his mind off of Zion. He wrote her a letter but was reluctant about sending it, so he kept it tucked in the back pocket of his prison uniform. A few weeks later, Bruh received a letter from Zion. The letter was written in royal purple ink and simply read, *"Keep ya head up . . . because soon, they gon' have to picture you rollin'.Love, Zion."*

The next letter mailed out was the one Bruh had been carrying around in his back pocket. His letter consisted of four lines: *"You got me feeling you. Listening for you. And wanting to be with you. Forever needing you in my corner, Bruh."*

For two years, this went on, back and forth. The last letter Bruh sent was a few days ago and it read,*"I'm comin' for you Ma . . . . Forever, Bruh."*

Bruh refocused his attention to the present situation, and continued to stare at Zion. She stood on her front porch, dressed in tight black capris, black and white throwback Pumas, and a fitted, black, rhinestone studded DKNY tank top. Her hair had grown since he last saw her and was now in a shoulder-length doobie with auburn tips. She was about 5'5" in height, which seemed shorter to Bruh than he last remembered.

Zion had her back to the street and three bags of groceries at her feet. Bruh was no longer content with being double-parked and watching her on the porch. He found the nearest parking space, which was on the far corner of the block.

Tossing his Hummer's keys in the air, Bruh walked on the porch and leaned against the metal railing. "Wassup, Ma?"

Scared as hell, Zion's first thoughts went to her .380 that she had in her top dresser drawer. Slowly she turned around and saw Bruh standing there, with broad shoulders. His tattoos seductively imprinted into his arms, worked the hell outta his mountains of muscles that only seemed to be missing wet kisses. His baseball cap barely showed his gray eyes. *"Got damn,"* Zion thought to herself, *"This nigga knows he fine."*

Bruh looked at Zion from head to foot; he imagined that even her drips of sweat would be sweet. Her skin was the color of apple-butter and her breasts seemed to be more than a mouthful. He could only imagine that the puffiness of her areolas would feel like silk against his lips. Thinking about how he could literally kiss her ass, Bruh reared back on the pole and pushed himself up, as if stopping his stare was a full-fledged effort.

"That's something new you picked up?" Zion said sarcastically.

"What?" Bruh asked.

"Staring."

"I only stare when I have something to say."

"Well say it, then," Zion urged.

"My eyes already did. You just have to learn to listen."

The sound of Bruh's DMX-like voice sent chills trampling through Zion's body like runaway slaves. "Bruh, please."

"Bruh, please?" he repeated with a smiled, "That's all I get? I been writing letters to you for two years and a nigga can't get no love?"

Afraid of melting in his arms, Zion reluctantly walked over to him and hugged him around his waist. He kissed her at the top of her head and said, "I missed you, Ma." After he released her from his embrace Bruh picked up her groceries in one sweep.

Zion tried to open the door and ended up dropping her keys. Nervousness ran all through her fingertips as she bit the inside of her jaw and picked up her keys. Zion slowly stood and caught a quick glimpse of the imprint of his dick and wondered if it would hurt going inside, being that she hadn't had any in a while.

Her satin panties became moist but Zion shook it off and reminded herself that she made a promise to never fuck with another hood. *They just too much trouble,* she thought to herself and after her son's father, Haas, she swore that she would leave hoods and drug dealers alone. Besides, Zion was a social worker for Child Protective Services and how would it look if she were dating a street nigga?

"Where's Seven?" Bruh asked, speaking of Zion's son. "With Haas?"

"Nigga, please," Zion hissed. "You know Haas ain't shit. Don't try and be slick and throw Haas' name out there to see where my head is at."

"Damn . . . fall back, Ma. I just asked. Haas is my man."

"If Haas is yo' man, then you need a better selection of friends. Seven is with my mother."

"What's up with you and Haas, that you about to take a nigga's head off?"

Zion slipped her sneakers off by the front door and walked into the kitchen. Bruh watched her ass grace the cotton material of her capris as her thighs moved. He placed the groceries in one hand, took the other hand, and pulled on the head of his dick. He needed to do that, in an effort to keep the hard on calm and the precome from sticking. Then he followed Zion into the kitchen.

"Haas and I don't deal like that, Bruh," Zion said while she unpacked her groceries. "I had to take a restraining order out on him."

"Get the fuck outta here." Bruh sat down on a barstool.

"Yes. He pulled his gun out on me because I caught him in the bed with a bitch."

"He did what?" Bruh said, shocked. "Niggas die for less than that." The vein on the side of his neck started thumpin', causing the tattoo etched there to rise. "When did this happen?"

"Two years ago."

"Before I got knocked?"

"The same day."

"Why didn't you tell me?"

"I don't know." Zion smirked as she continued to put the groceries away, "I guess I was scared to say anything."

"Scared to tell me?" Bruh frowned. "What the fuck is that?"

"I don't know, Bruh." Zion hunched her shoulders. "I just didn't say nothin'. Fuck that nigga. He can't be that bad, at least in your book. You still got him on the street."

"Him being on the street got to do with cake, trust and believe it ain't got shit to do with love."

"Humph, and don't we know niggas go hard for that cake."

"Ai'ight," Bruh chuckled, "this conversation that you think you about to have with me is a wrap. So how's work?"

Zion grabbed a box of grits and threw it at him. Bruh caught it and started laughing. "Damn, girl. I ain't come home from prison to be abused."

"Niggas." Zion sighed.

"Yo," Bruh smirked, taken aback. "What, you servin' the block or somethin', how you gon' be the wife talkin' hood rat shit?"

"The wife?" Zion laughed, pointing her finger, "There go that bullshit."

Bruh shook his head, "Goddamn, y'all broads got some hot ass mouths."

"Y'all?" Zion sucked her teeth. "Look, don't be comparing me to Tomika."

"I would never compare you to Tomika. I actually wanna be with you."

Zion took a deep breath and looked at Bruh. "*Paleeze,* because you are this short of telling a lie. You were diggin' Tomika because she was fast paced and you were beatin' the street. She got pregnant and yo' ass got stuck. You didn't wanna fuck with me because I was too much of a square for you. But now that you've gotten knocked, you don't wanna repeat that shit. So you're looking to calm down by running to me. But you can forget that shit, cause this ain't where it's at."

Bruh didn't respond. Instead, he stood up behind her, and pressed his dick against the split of her ass. He reached over her shoulder and removed a box of cereal from her hand.

"What are you doing?" Zion said, trying to keep her nipples from getting hard.

Bruh turned her around and sat back down on the barstool. "Come here," he pulled her toward him. Zion climbed on the barstool and straddled him.

"Yo, I missed you. And that's my word." Bruh kissed her neck. "Believe me, Ma, the way I feel has nothing to do with Haas, Tomika, or with me tryin' to flex no muscle, or no fuckin' game."

Zion wanted to get up but the heat from Bruh's hard-on felt too good. "Bruh. Please. I'm not taking it there. And this doesn't have shit to with Haas or Tomika. I don't want no nigga in the street. Finally, I'm out of school, and I'm just trying to do me."

"Let me do that,"Bruh insisted, with a soft kiss on her lips.

"Let me up." Zion protested, even as she responded to his kisses.

"Why?" Bruh slipped his tongue in and out of her mouth, circled it above her upper lip, and then kissed her on the lips again. "Damn, I missed you." He sucked on her neck. "You know how long I been wanting to do this?"

"Bruh," Zion moaned, "For real, you need to leave. We gotta stop."

"Why?" He was now biting her nipples through her shirt and leaving wet rings behind.

"Because . . . my mother will be here any minute with my son."

"Ai'ight . . ." Bruh squeezed her ass. "When you want me to come back?

"Monday."

"Monday? It's Saturday, what did Sunday do? Leave the rest of the week behind. Come on, ma, don't play ya man."

"My man?" she smirked.

"Ai'ight, whatever," he snapped. "What's your work schedule?"

"It's like most, nine to five."

"Bet. I'll see you around six."

"Just so you know, ain't shit goin' on."

"Look," Zion climbed off Bruh's lap and led him to the front door. "This is my house; I don't need no nigga to buy it. I can afford the mortgage. That BMW 325I may be small, but I floss in it, 'cause I paid for it. I got money in the bank, and my son doesn't want for shit. So, what I need a nigga for? Some dick? Please, I can play with my own pussy."

"Let me watch." Bruh licked his lips.

"Boy please."

Bruh turned away from the front door, "Let me taste it."

Zion's heart started pumping harder, she couldn't believe that he'd said that. "What?"

"Stop playin' me."

"Stop playin' you?" Zion bit the corner of her lip.

Bruh pulled her close and whispered into her hair, "You smell so good. I know it taste like honey. You ever taste it? I wanna see you play with it."

"Bruh would you stop . . . please . . ."

"I want to," Bruh responded while taking her shirt out of her pants and running his hands under it and across her nipples. "But I can't."

"You can," Zion moaned, "Please . . . you have to . . . I can't do this. Tomika and I are friends."

"But I don't wanna be with her. I want you and I don't wanna pretend anymore."

"Bruh please." Zion felt Bruh unzip her capris and slip his hands in her pants, "I'm not in the mood for no jail-house-everybody-need-love shit. OK?"

"Stop frontin' me." Bruh caressed her clit. "Damn this shit is thick . . ." He played in her wetness.

Zion's entire pussy, from the tip of the clit to the bottom of the lips, was going through convulsions. All she could do was bite harder on her bottom lip.

"I know you wanna scream." He took her right hand and placed it in her pants, guiding her fingers across her clit and into her wet pussy, "See how warm it is?" He moved her fingers in a circular motion, "See how thick it is? Damn," Bruh kissed Zion on the lips, "I want you to play with the clit while I'm hittin' this shit."

"You are so nasty," she complained.

"Take off your clothes."

"No," she said taking her hand out of her pants. "Now stop." She backed away, causing his hands to come out of her pants.

Bruh licked her wetness off his fingers then pulled her back close to him. "I want you to talk to me while I'm hittin' it." He picked Zion up off the floor and she wrapped her legs around his waist. While she held onto his neck, Bruh was able to ease her up enough to get her shirt above her head. Anxious to suck her breast, he lifted her bra and, just like he thought, the areola felt like silk.

No longer wanting to pretend that she didn't wanna fuck her girlfriend's man, Zion melted in Bruh's arms. He stopped sucking and kissing her breast and said, "I thought your son and mother were on their way?"

"My mother moved to Atlanta and Seven's spending the summer with her. I lied." Zion moaned, laying her head in the crook of his neck.

"I figured as much." Bruh placed her back on the floor and she unbuckled his belt. Once his pants were undone, Zion got her first glimpse of the dick.

"You want some of that?" Bruh asked.

"Yes," she whispered.

Zion led Bruh into her bedroom. By now she'd pulled her bra back over her breasts. She closed the mini blinds, lit some candles, and turned the light off. Although it was still early afternoon, this part of the house stayed dark. She turned on a Sade CD and played "Your Love is King."

Bruh was suave although he was anxious to fuck her. He slowly removed his clothes, never taking his eyes off her. By the time he took his boxer's off, Zion could've sworn that the crock in his dick was speaking a language that only her pussy could understand. Bruh placed his guns on Zion's dresser, and walked toward her. "Z," he said, placing his arms around her waist, "The candles and Sade are cool but I wanna freak you. I wanna hear some music that makes me bang the shit out you."

"And you think you can handle that?" Zion stepped out of his embrace and changed the CD to a club mix. The song "Jack Ya Body" by Steve "Silk" Hurley was playing.

"Turn that up. All the way up," Bruh said. "Now . . . turn the lights back on."

Zion stopped immediately in her tracks and thought about the pudginess of her belly and the stretch marks she had from being pregnant with her son. "I don't wanna turn the lights on."

"Why not?" Bruh asked, pulling at his dick.

"Because . . . I'm shy . . . about my body . . . my stomach . . . and I have stretch marks," Zion said, somewhat embarrassed. The CD player was knockin' and if you didn't know any better, you would've thought that they were in a nightclub, as the house version of Me'lisa Morgan's "Still In Love" came thrusting through the surround sound.

Bruh walked over to Zion. His body was so fine that he should've been arrested for having it. He flicked the lights on and said, "Stop it, right now. I'ma fuck the shit outta you, because I'm feeling you like that. I don't give a damn about your stomach, your stretch marks, or anything else you feel is outta place. My dick is hard because you turn me on both mentally and physically. You're beautiful, and I don't give a fuck about nothing else. Now come here."

Zion walked so close to Bruh that she was practically in his chest. He bent down on his knees and kissed her from the tip of her toes and slowly up her thighs. She stood there, breathing heavy, and shaking. The club CD felt like it was bangin' in the base of her clit and she could feel it thump as each beat slipped through the speakers.

Bruh's hands moved like snakes up Zion's body. He kissed the inner parts of her thighs, going from one to the other. Then he opened her pussy lips with his hands, starred at her clit and kissed it. "Damn, this shit is nice and fat. I wanna see you play with it." He grabbed her right hand and placed her index finger on her clit. "Come on ma, let me see."

Zion softly caressed her clit, as Bruh held her pussy lips open, nervously rubbing her fingers all over it.

"Don't be nervous," Bruh assured her. "Close you eyes and pretend I'm suckin' it."

Zion closed her eyes and dipped her fingers into her slit. Afterwards she smeared her own juices all over her clit. Trembles started to shoot down her legs, causing her knees to become weak. As the nut began to build she swiftly moved her fingers in a circular motion.

This was driving Bruh insane. *Goddamn,* he thought to himself.

As her juices started running between her thighs, Bruh started licking them off.Zion started to moan uncontrollably and her clit felt like silk between her fingertips. Slowly Bruh worked his way up her thigh to the creases of her pussy, licking the outline of it with his tongue. He tickled her pubic hairs as he began to suck her fingers. The same fingers that were stroking her clit. After sucking Zion's juices from her fingertips, Bruh placed his tongue on her clit, kissing, teasing, and gently pulling it between his teeth.

"I'm about to come," she moaned.

"Put your legs over my shoulders," he commanded.

"How am I going to do that?" Zion was confused.

"I'ma hold you up."

Zion placed her legs over Bruh's shoulders; he supported her back with his hands. With her pussy directly in his face, he took his tongue and started licking her pussy all over, then he zoned in on her clit. Instantly she started screaming!

"It's dripping," Bruh mumbled into the lips of her pussy.

"Dripping like what?" Zion moaned.

"Like honey." He removed her legs from his shoulders. "Every time you come I want you to say to me, 'Bruh, its dripping like honey.'"

Zion agreed as Bruh gently laid her down on the carpeted floor. The club CD was still bangin' and the song playing now was, "When Can Our Love Begin" by Kimara Lovelace . . . the CD pumped . . . *"When can our love begin . . . I'm tired of being friends. It only takes one kiss . . . and everything is gonna change . . ."* And on it went. Bruh took Zion's legs and lifted her lower body leaving her shoulders and a small portion of her back to rest on the floor. He was now standing as he took his pretty honey-colored dick and slowly rubbed it against her vaginal lips. "You want me to fuck you?" Bruh demanded to know.

"Yes." Zion moaned.

"I'll fuck you on one condition." He used the head of his dick to part her lips gently.

"What's the condition?"

"That you tell me when it's dripping."

"Like honey?"

"Like honey," Bruh moaned, pushing his dick all the way in.

Just as Zion thought, his dick hurt going in. It felt like it was reaching for her stomach.

Bruh could feel her vaginal tightness and he wanted to stew in it, but he knew that he was well endowed and it would only be a matter of time before the tightness would give way. As he continued to pump into her, he could feel her tightness breaking up.

Zion was in sheer ecstasy as Bruh was grinding so hard that she was lifted off the floor with each stroke. As each stroke slipped in and out of her dripping wet vaginal canal the slurping sounds of his dick pounding into it seemed to hold a conversation all its own.

Bruh was banging her back out, causing Zion to stutter while she screamed, "Bru-Bru-Bruh-Bruhhhhhhh!"

"What is it?" He slapped her on the ass.

"Bruh," she moaned again, trying not to stutter.

"Say it!" He demanded.

"Oh God! It's dripping!" she screamed.

"Dripping like what?" he held his come back so that they could explode together.

"Like honey!" Zion screamed, and that's when they came. Bruh took his dick out and came on all over her stomach. The come slid down her belly and around her waist, before dripping onto the carpeted floor.

Bruh collapsed on top of Zion and kissed the sweat off her forehead.

* * * *

When Bruh left Zion's it was eight o'clock in the evening. He had been there all day and before he left, she gave him two more dripping honey episodes.

He looked at the time and knew that Sef was going to be pissed, knowing that the routine of Bruh collecting the money was supposed to resume today. Sef didn't want Bruh to miss one beat of the hustle, especially after being away for two years. Bruh had to let niggas know that he was back on the grind, pushin' weight, and handling his shit. Bruh assured Zion that he would be back in the morning, before she went to work.

As soon as Bruh walked out the door Zion swore that her pussy would be sore for days. She relaxed on the bed and sudden chills ran through her body as she began to think about how tight Bruh's lips gripped her clit. In an effort to keep from masturbating herself back into the memory of being fucked on the floor, she stuffed a pillow between her legs and turned over to sleep. As soon as Zion was relaxed enough she began to drift off to sleep. The moment that she slipped into a dream, her doorbell rang. It was Tomika and Milan.

Milan stood next to her mother. She looked identical to her father, except she had Tomika's chocolate complexion. She had Bruh's gray eyes and was a little chubbier than the average four year old. Her hair was zigzag parted down the middle and styled into two shoulder-length, double-strand twist ponytails. She wore a pink Nike short set, rocking from side to side and looking up in the sky as if she didn't have a care in the world.

Bruh had been literally seconds away from missing Tomika. He hopped in his Hummer and drove a little ways down the block before he thought to check his neck for passion marks, because Zion had been biting the shit out of him. Seeing that he had only a small one on his chest, he was straight. He slid in some Jay-Z, and pulled off again.

"Busted nigga!" Sef yelled.

Bruh smiled, "Nigga please. Busted for what?"

Sef glared at Bruh from the driver sear of his fully loaded, sterling silver, Nav. He smiled and said, "Wipe ya lip; you got come all over ya face."

"Yeah, ai'ight." Bruh chuckled, but wondered for a brief moment if that were true. He nixed it off. "What's up? I was just coming to check you."

"Yeah, that's why I'm here. I started looking for you earlier and then I thought, who did this ma'-fucker say he was tryna wife when he hit the street? Zion. And wouldn't you know, I was right. Here you are."

All Bruh could do was smile.

"Was the pussy good?" Sef asked.

Bruh gave Sef a serious look and said, "Don't even take it there."

"Oh shit, she must be that bitch. Straight wife material," Sef shouted. "My nigga."

Laughing at Sef and not wanting to comment any further, Bruh took off and headed toward Lil Bricks, where his Ironbound section runners hung out in the courtyard. Sef laughed as well and followed behind him.

When Bruh and Sef pulled up on the corner of Lil' Bricks, they parked their trucks so that they weren't so visible to the courtyard. Bruh saw some of his runners, Moe, Wu, and Mumeen, playin' a game of C-Lo.

The night air was thick with puffs of purple haze. The traffic was relatively quiet, with the exception of a few speeders and stolen cars racing through the block. There were a few crack heads standing around and watching Bruh's runners, trying desperately to figure out how they were gon' step up, snatch some cash, and run off with their lives.

A few of the baller jump-offs, were sitting on the bench adjacent to the one Mumeen had his foot on.

Seeing that not much had changed in the time that he'd been in prison, freedom began to sink into Bruh's mind in different variables. He stood still and only moving his eyes from side to side he looked around the courtyard for Haas. The vision that Zion painted of Haas pulling a gun on her, made Bruh's hands thirsty for the pull of his trigger. He felt for the butt of the gun tucked in his waist.

For a quick moment Bruh thought about setting Haas up to be kidnapped, dumped in a trunk, and finished off, or perhaps hung from the telephone pole. However, as quickly as that thought entered his mind, it left.

Mumeen stood with one foot on the courtyard bench and the other foot on the ground; hundred-dollar bills were swept under his feet as he rolled the dice.

"Hurry up nigga, damn!" Wu, who was dying to get in the game, yelled at Mumeen.

Mumeen looked at Wu and pulled up his right sweat pants leg, and revealed the butt of his gun. "Better be easy nigga." Then he cracked up laughing.

"That's my money, nigga?" Bruh said, walking up on Mumeen.

"Oh shit!" Mumeen turned around. He dropped the dice and a hundred-dollar bill to the ground, "Where this ma'fucker come from?"Mumeen and Bruh exchanged some dap. He looked at Bruh and said, "This the ma'fuckin man right here!"

Bruh smiled as his eyes still searched for Haas. He gave Mumeen a pound and asked, "Where's Haas?"

"Haas?" Mumeen was surprised. He squinted

his eyes and looked at Sef. "You ain't tell 'em that this nigga missin'?"

"What the fuck you mean, missin'?" Bruh was taken aback. He looked Sef up and down. "What the hell is goin' on?"

"Haas," Sef said, folding his arms across his chest, "started making the D.C. runs"

"What happen to lil' shortie . . . Gwen?" Bruh asked.

"That bitch got knocked up. And you know once a bitch gets pregnant, it's a wrap. 5-0 mention taking that baby and everybody's going down."

Bruh looked at Sef in disbelief. "That nigga should've never been responsible for makin' no runs without consulting me first, whether I was in prison or not. Now finish the rest of the story." Bruh tried to keep his nostrils from flaring but he couldn't help it.

"He went to D.C. last week to make the switch with the money and the work. Well, they made the switch, but when D.C. went to break down the car, there was no work to be found. Nobody's seen Haas since."

"What's D.C. saying?" The vein in Bruh's neck was about to explode.

"What the fuck you mean, *what they sayin*? You been locked up that long?" Sef looked Bruh up and down. "It's a wrap, for Haas' ass. Er'body want that nigga done."

"You might wanna take that down, son," Bruh said to Sef, arching his thick eyebrows, "Furthermore, how much money was it?"

"Two twenty-five," Mu answered.

"Two hundred and twenty-five grand?" Bruh's eyes widened.

"Yeah," Mu confirmed.

"Find that nigga." Bruh demanded. "Now!"

"Bruh," Sef raised his voice and pointed his finger, "I told yo' ass Haas was a greedy nigga from the start and you still put him on—"

"Hold up, my man," Bruh pounded his chest. "Who the fuck you really talkin' to? What, you forgot yo' ma'fuckin' place? I ain't one of these lil' niggas out here. You better get the fuck back in line, take your position, and knock that shit down."

"Whatever yo," Sef waved his hand.

"You testin' me, and in the street?" Had it been anybody else but Sef, Bruh would'a beat their ass, but because he had love for Sef, Bruh figured he would make his point with words. Bruh got so close to Sef that his spit was sprinkling his eyes, "You fuckin' crazy? You know what? I don't even see you right now. 'Cause you done fuckin' lost yourself. All you need to do, is find that nigga.

Now get the fuck out my face!"

Sef stepped back.

"Haas is beggin' to be murked. Just say the word," Mumeen said, "and it's done."

"Naw," Bruh said, "It's gon' be my pleasure to see about the nigga." Bruh looked at Sef. "Make sure his ass is found. One."

They all parted ways in the courtyard. Sef stayed with the other runners and Bruh went to see about his daughter.

Crossing over Springfield Avenue, Bruh couldn't believe Sef. "I'ma have to watch that nigga," Bruh said to himself, while calling Tomika's grandmother to tell her that he was on his way to get Milan.

"She ain't here, Bruh," Tomika's grandmother, Ms. Mae, said. "Tomika said that she was going away and that she was taking Milan with her."

Bruh's heart felt like it had stopped. "What? Where did they go? When did they leave?"

"They left this afternoon. Tomika didn't say where she was going. She just said that she was leaving."

"No disrespect, Ms. Mae, but you telling the truth, aren't you?"

"Boy!" Ms. Mae screamed, "You calling me a liar? One thing I don't do is get into y'all's mess! And boy, I hope that you don't get back out there in that street. You got a chile. You done missed two years of her life already!"

"I'm sorry, Ms. Mae," Bruh said. He didn't mean to upset her.

"Yeah, you sho' right!" Ms. Mae hung up.

Bruh slammed his hand against the steering wheel and then he dialed Tomika's cell phone.

"Hello," Tomika answered.

"Where my ma'fuckin daughter at?!" Bruh screamed into the phone.

"She's where she's been for the last two years, with me."

"Bring my daughter home!"

"Nigga, please. You ain't shit! All you care about is the ma'fuckin' pavement. Chasin' that paper. You gave me a month to leave, so I bounced! Now what? You'll see your daughter when I say that you can see her and not before. Now take that and kick rocks with it, bitch! You gon' try and play me. Do you even know who I am?"

"I know you better have my ma'fuckin' daughter home when I get there!"

"Whatever," Tomika said, yawning. "Now suck my dick, ya Kool-Aid bitch. One." And she hung up on him.

Bruh called her back for what felt like at least a million times. Every time he called Tomika would hang up on him, causing him to feel like he was going crazy.

He couldn't believe this. He went by everybody's house that he knew Tomika could run to and came up with nothing. His heart felt as if it had collapsed with the thought about never seeing his daughter again. He began to feel anxious. He spent hours looking for and calling Tomika, and never receiving an answer. "My right hand to God," Bruh said, holding tears back, "that bitch gon' make me kill her."

Not being able to take the constant riding up and down the blocks, he called Zion.

"Yo, what up?" Bruh said to her when she answered the phone.

"What's wrong, baby?" Zion said hearing the stress in his voice.

"Yo I feel like I'm going crazy, Tomika won't let me see Milan." He had to stop talking because his anger made him feel as if the lump in his throat would explode.

"Come see me," Zion said.

"You know it's late as hell, Ma."

"Time never mattered before."

"I'm on my way."

Biting the inside of his cheek, he couldn't catch the tears that slipped from his eyes as he thought about snapping Tomika's neck.

Before going to Zion's he stopped by his house and grabbed some gear. When he got to Zion's house he parked in front, walked on to the porch, and rang the bell.

It was midnight and Zion answered the door as if it were noon. She wore a pair of fridge bottom short-shorts and a sky blue sleeveless tee. Her hair was pulled back into a ponytail. Her smile glistened as she opened the door. Despite the feeling Bruh was carrying in his heart, his dick got hard, at the sight of her thick thighs. "You may as well not even turn around," he walked up close to her, "'cause if you move and I get a glimpse of that ass . . ."

"Boy, please." Before Zion could say anymore, a little girl ran up behind her and grabbed her from behind. "Zion! Zion! Is that my daddy! Is that my daddy, like you said?" Now the little girl had her head between Zion's legs while peeking up at Bruh.

When Bruh looked down, he saw a four-year-old chocolate version of himself. "You look just like your picture, Daddy," Milan said to Bruh.

Bruh couldn't believe it. He hadn't seen his daughter since she was two and he knew she couldn't have remembered how he looked. He was expecting to meet a little girl who had to be reintroduced to him, not one who already knew him.

"Come around here," Zion said to Milan. Milan walked around Zion. "Remember all those pictures that I showed you of your daddy?" Zion said.

"Yes," Milan responded.

"Well then, here he is."

Milan walked up to Bruh. Bruh bent down and Milan gave him a hug. "You don't look nothin' like Haas," she said.

"Haas?" Bruh said taken aback. "What?"

"Sometimes," Zion said, "Sef would send him to take Tomika money while you were away."

"Yeah, ai'ight. You know I ain't quite feeling that."

"Good." Zion rubbed his back while he held Milan in his arms, "'cause that ain't what you need to be feeling. Just enjoy the innocence of your daughter."

Falling deeper in love with Zion, Bruh stood up, with Milan at his side and kissed Zion on the forehead. "Where's Tomika?" he asked.

"She went to Atlanta and asked me to keep Milan. She told me that she wasn't going to let you see her, which is why I was glad that she asked me to keep her. I didn't wanna see you hurt. Look," Zion said, "spend some time with Milan; she'll be here for two days."

Although it was late, Milan and Bruh stayed

up for at least two more hours playing. While playing with her, Bruh learned that Milan knew how to spell her name, how to count, and her alphabet.

Bruh and Milan ended up falling asleep on the couch. It was three o'clock in the morning when Zion tapped him on the shoulder.

"Let me lay her down." Zion lifted Milan off Bruh's chest and carried her into Seven's room.Once she put Milan in bed, Zion walked back into the living room and said to Bruh, "Come here. I wanna talk to you."

Bruh followed her into her bedroom. He sat on the edge of the bed and removed his boots and jeans, leaving only his boxers and wife beater on. Although it was dark, with the exception of the small wicker lamp that Zion had glowing, his muscles seemed to reflect sunshine.

Bruh lay back on the bed with his feet planted on the floor and motioned for Zion to come and lay beside him. She complied, placed her head against his chest and inhaled the sweet smell of his cologne.

"Bruh," Zion said into his chest while running her hands across his nipples, "What's up with this, with us? What's next?"Afraid of being rejected she added, "Whatever you decide, I'm cool with it. I don't know if I want a relationship, anyway. However, I do know that I will not deal with you fucking Tomika and me at the same time. So if you want Tomika, then its all good, we can still be friends."

"You finished?" Bruh said, slightly annoyed. He'd been rubbing his hands all over her ass, but as soon as she said, "We can still be friends . . ." he took his hands off, "Don't play me, Ma. I'm not in the mood. If you got some shit to ask me, then just ask me."

"I already said what I had to say." Zion lifted her head from his chest to look at him.

Bruh pulled her on top of him and sat her up so that she was now straddled across his lap. "Don't interrupt me again," he said, "especially after you ask me a question; give me a chance to answer. *Now* . . . what was that slick shit you said about me and you being friends?"

"Just that. We can still be friends. "

"Ma," Bruh said seriously, "after the way I fucked you today, we could never be friends. If I didn't want you, I would've never fucked you like you that. Fuckin' a bitch you don't want is for tricks and hoes."

"You calling me a trick?" Zion snapped.

"No baby," Bruh reassured her as he resumed feeling on her ass. "I was just using that as an expression."

"Don't use it with me."

"Ai'ight, my bad," Bruh said apologetically. "But listen, I'm feeling you and I'm feeling you to the point where I feel like I'm in love with you, Ma, and that's on my word. I know I'm a street nigga but I'ma good man."

"But I'm Tomika's friend."

"I know you're Tomika's friend. But where does that leave me? I been thinking about you and wanting to be with you for three years now, and that's way too long."

"What about Tomika?" Zion moved slightly so that his hard-on could hit on her clit.

"Tomika did me dirty for a minute, but she's Milan's mother, so I'ma try to do the right thing because I gotta take care of my daughter, but I can't stand Tomika's ass. Believe dat. I told her earlier that I didn't want nothing to do with her."

"Before or after you fuck her?" Zion said with a serious look on her face.

"Go 'head with that." Bruh tried brushing Zion off.

"Did you fuck her?"

Knowing that Tomika was by Zion's earlier Bruh didn't know whether to tell Zion the truth or not so he said, "What did she tell you?"

"Don't be slick nigga. Did you fuck her?"

"Hell no," Bruh lied, blinking his eyes. He glared at Zion's face to see if she believed him.

"You're lying," Zion spat at him, "Tomika told me you did, so why lie?"

"Zion." Bruh sat up and looked her directly in the face. She was still sitting on his lap, so he pulled her closer, "I'm feeling the hell outta you. I already told you, you that bitch, claim that shit. It's all about you. Don't make Tomika a problem, I don't want her, I want you. Period."

"Then when is she leaving your house?"

"I told her that she had two weeks to leave."

Zion took a deep breath; she wanted badly to believe Bruh, "Don't play me, Bruh. If I give you my heart then you gotta take care of it."

"Why wouldn't I?" Bruh gave her a light kiss.

"I don't know. But if you fuck with me, I'ma catch a case."

Bruh mushed her head slightly and said, "Ma, you're too much of a square to be catching a case. But I feel you. Just know that a nigga like me will shoot a ma'fucker without hesitation, so if you don't fuck with Haas now, don't fuck with him on my watch."

"Now that we have a mutual understanding," Zion laughed "I want you to know that I've been thinking about this dick all day."

Bruh smiled, relieved that he had glossed over his lie. "Yeah? You been thinking about the dick or thinking about me?"

"Both."

"You should'a called and told me."

"Were you thinking about me?" Zion asked.

"Yeah," he kissed her on the lips. "And my dick has been hard as hell."

"Why didn't you call me and tell me?"

"Because I had shit to do and calling you would have took me there. Plus, I wanted to come up in you, not on my front seat."

"I want you to come up in me, too."

"You want me to fuck you right now, don't you?"

"My pussy is wet for it," Zion gave him a sly smile.

"*Your* pussy or *my* pussy?" Bruh smiled.

"Only yours."

"It better be."

Zion's pussy throbbed as she started grinding against Bruh slightly. "I got somethin' for you." She pulled his wife beater over his head.

"What you got for Daddy?"

Zion laughed, "Ai'ight now, cut the daddy shit, cuz that sounds so nasty."

"Whatever, Ma," Bruh smiled. "What you wanna show ya man?"

"My man, huh?" Zion said, more to herself

than to him.

Zion walked over to the lamp and turned it off, then turned on another lamp that was on her computer desk. The lamp had a red light bulb in it, so the light added a reddish hue to the darkness in the room. Flipping on the CD player, she decided to play an old CD by Lady Saw called "Passion." She kicked it to track number two. "Can you dance to Dub?"

"Hell yeah." He looked at her and imagined that the music was melting into her thighs.

"Stand up then," Zion ordered.

Bruh stood up while the music pumped, *"Can you whine . . . Can you pump the pussy until me cry . . ."* He stood behind Zion and she started to whine against his hard dick. Her thick thighs and short-shorts created just enough friction against the soft cotton of his light blue boxers. His dick was so hard that the split in his boxers started to rise.

Zion was grinding as hard as she could against his dick. The Jamaican that she had in her from her mother's family was enough to drive even the hardest nigga crazy. "Fuck," Bruh mumbled to himself as Zion bent down and threw her ass against his shaft. He placed his hands around her waist and they both began to grind to the music.

Zion turned around, "Lay down," she said, "I been thinking about the next time I would be seeing this dick since you left."

"Yeah," Bruh said as he laid on the bed and allowed her to slip his boxers off. "What did you wanna do when you saw it?" The music was still pumping.

"I was thinking," Zion said, as she removed her clothes with full confidence, "about how I wanted to fuck the shit out of you."

"Z," Bruh laughed, "you straight undercover . . . but baby, Milan is in the other room."

"So?" She frowned, "The door is locked and she's sleep."

"But baby," Bruh felt her now naked ass and ran his hand between her butt cheeks, "we been fuckin' all day."

"No, you fucked me, earlier. Now, I'ma fuck you. But you gotta play along."

Bruh's dick stood straight in the air with a slight crook in it. "You got a nigga dick about to bust. Wassup?"

Zion got off his lap and walked over to the nightstand. She took out a blindfold and said, "You gotta wear this.

"A blindfold, Z? Oh, *hell* no."

"You gotta play along," she teased.

Bruh took a deep breath and said, "Ai'ight." He laid back on the bed but Zion said "Not the bed . . . the chair . . . over here."

Playing along and happy that Zion was even

more undercover than he thought, he sat in the chair and let her blindfold him. "Another thing," she said to him, "you can't touch."

"Can't touch? Can't touch what?"

"You can't touch me, just let me do you."Zion turned up the CD player just a notch and this time Lady Saw sang, " . . . *Do you like it when I get X-rated Ba'byyy . . . Do you like it when I get X-tra naked . . . Darling. .You like the bumpin' and grindin'.*"And then the Reggae artist Tanya was mixed into the song and she sang, *"Have you ever wondered what makes a woman come . . . Have you ever asked her if she likes the way you do it . . . A woman must be satisfied before you say you're done . . . You're not ready for this yet boy . . ."*

"Z," Bruh sat blindfolded as the bass of the Caribbean music pounded through him. "As fat as that ass is, and you expect me not to touch? Come on now, be fair."

"I am." Zion opened his legs and slid to her knees. By the time Bruh started to comment, she had his dick in her mouth. The ridges of his balls massaged her chin as she made her way down to kiss and suck those as well. Bruh tried not to scream; he thought he was going to lose his mind. He ran his hand through her hair. Zion snapped, "I told you not to touch. Keep it up and I'ma tie your hands together."

Bruh laughed in disbelief as she commenced to

sucking his dick, catching him totally off guard.

Zion stroked the veins on the sides of his dick with her tongue, back and forth, dripping juices from her mouth all over the head. She licked the sides of the head and circled the mushroom-like shape of it, and licked underneath and the sides. Once she had absorbed as much of the head as Bruh could tolerate, Zion slowly eased the dick into her mouth one inch at a time. She placed it on the side of her mouth and hit him off with a jawbreaker. Bruh was losing his mind!

Quickly Bruh felt himself rising to his peak. Zion could feel his stomach muscles contracting, so she stopped sucking his dick and went to licking his balls only. Then she slid her wet tongue up and down the inner parts of his thighs. For a split second, she stopped long enough to pop a Halls cough drop in her mouth and let it melt. Her fingertips were caressing his dick so well, that Bruh started to feel himself being forced into an orgasm.

As soon as most of the cough drop melted, Zion blew across Bruh's hard dick and took the shaft into her cool mouth. He started moaning her name to the point of almost screaming. Not being able to hold the nut back any longer, Bruh exploded, and drippings of his creamy white come slid down Zion's throat and out the sides of her mouth.After she swallowed and wiped her mouth with the back of her hand, Zion stood up, sat on his lap and started kissing him. Bruh felt his way to her breast and said, "Let me suck it."

Zion brushed his hands down and said, "Didn't I say you couldn't touch?"

"Put it in my mouth, then," he begged.

Zion complied. She took her two D cups and slid both nipples across his lips. Bruh kissed them in fast strokes as she ran them across his lips repeatedly. When she stopped caressing his lips with her nipples, he took one between his teeth and sucked it as if he were a newborn just learning to latch on. He was sucking them so well that Zion hadn't realized that he had slipped his hand underneath her and was playing with her clit.

"I swear," Bruh said, still sucking her breast, "this is the only pussy I ever wanted to taste this bad. Come on Z, take the blindfold off."

"No," she said. Zion turned her back to him in a reverse cowboy and slid her pussy down on his hard dick. Having to get use to a big dick all over again, Zion didn't make a sound, although her pussy ached just a little from his dick going in. After Bruh was all the way in, she gave up fighting and let his hands run all over her ass.

Zion grabbed his ankles and bounced up and down on his dick, like a slave picking fresh cotton. Bruh felt as if his dick were disappearing in an ocean of nothing but hot and dripping wet pussy. This was the shit! Tanya and Lady Saw mixed together were helping Zion to turn Bruh out. Bruh was sure that once Zion was done fucking him that he would know the true meaning of being pussy whipped.At this point, he was feeling like he had no control over his own body. The only thing missing was some ganja.

Before Bruh could retract his pelvic muscles, the nut had already eased out and was working its way to explode into Zion.

"Z," Bruh said, "this is the shit!"

Zion didn't answer right away because she was too busy trying to get herself together after coming so strong. Bruh could feel Zion's come oozing onto his thighs and he said, "Why didn't you tell me when it was dripping?"

"Because it just happened."

"Nothing just happens, take this damn blind fold off me! If I don't get to lick the clit once I'ma go crazy!"

Zion removed the blindfold. Bruh looked at her and felt in his heart that he could be with her forever. He caressed her clit while sliding two fingers inside of her.

"Wait, wait baby," Zion said as he circled his fingers in and out of her pussy. "I got something for you." She grabbed her housecoat. Conscious of Milan being asleep in her son's room, she was careful not to walk through the house naked. When she came back, she had a bowl of warm honey, "Since you love to talk about honey so much lets see what you can do."

"You'se a freak, " Bruh smiled, loving every bit of it. He took the bowl of honey from her hand. Zion layed down on the bed and he poured the honey all over her breasts and dripped it slowly down the center of her belly. Dying to know what her clit would taste like with honey in his mouth, he licked some of the honey off her belly and then commenced to licking the outside of her pussy before zoning in on the inside. "What does it taste like?" Zion asked.

"Like honey," Bruh replied, "It taste just like honey . . ."

Slowly he licked her pussy until it rose and fell in his mouth, leaving a trail of come sliding down his chin. Once he had licked the clit all he could, Bruh poured more honey between her cleavage and said, "Hold your breasts together." Once Zion did that Bruh slid his dick in between.

Seeing the honey glowing on the tip of his beautiful dick, Zion held her head up and began to lick the honey off every time the tip came near her mouth. This drove Bruh crazy; he had never been on the verge of busting so many nuts in one night.

After they finished freaking each other, topping it all off with doggy style, tossed salad, 69, and Zion riding Bruh, they layed down, and stewed in each other's juices.

As soon as Bruh began to think about asking Zion what she thought of anal sex, his cell phone rang. It was Sef.

"Speak," Bruh answered. Zion lay with her head against his chest, wondering if that was Tomika on his phone. "You found him? Atlanta? Tonight, he should be back? Ai'ight. One."

When Bruh hung up Zion was looking him dead in the face. "Who'll be back?"

"Let's get this straight, so we have an understanding," Bruh said to Zion. He looked in her eyes and stroking her hair. "I'm not ever putting you in no street shit. You understand? That's not how you are and I don't want or need you in the middle of that."

"But Bruh, I love you and I can't be wondering if you gon' come home or not, if the police got you or if somebody killed you."

"Zion I just came home from prison; I'm not trying to go back. But there are some things I have to deal with when it comes to the street."

"Like what?"

He rolled on top of her and said, "You know I'm not telling you that. So stop talking and kiss me."

Zion looked at the clock and said, "Its nine o'clock in the morning, we have a child here. Get up and get dressed, so you can take her out to eat."

"Me? What about all of us?"

"Bruh," Zion got out of the bed. "You need to spend time with your daughter alone. I know her already and now she needs to know you."

"Ai'ight. You're right. But I need you to tell me something before I go. What's up with us? We in this together or what? I'm trying to wife you, Ma."

Zion looked at Bruh and said, "This is it, baby, and I ain't goin' nowhere, for nothing or for nobody."

Bruh got out of bed as well. Seeing that Milan must've been exhausted because she was still asleep, Bruh and Zion took a shower together and hit each other off under hot streams of water. By the time they carefully stepped out of the bathroom, one at a time, Milan was in the living room watching television.

They went into the bedroom and got dressed for the day. Afterward, Zion washed and dressed Milan, and explained to her that she would be going out with her daddy for a while. Before Bruh left Zion told him to grab the spare the keys from the kitchen table.

Bruh took Milan to breakfast at Je's. After breakfast, they caught a movie, then went to the park and the toy store. By the time he came back to Zion's, Milan was sleepy and Zion was napping on the couch.

Bruh woke Zion up with a kiss after he layed Milan down to sleep. Zion smiled and said, "The prince has arrived?"

"Yeah, baby," he said, kissing her again, "It's your prince. Or better yet your king." She sat up on the couch and smiled at him. "Who's the chick sleep in Seven's room?" Bruh asked.

"My cousin. She has an attitude with her boyfriend so she came by here to sleep tonight. It's OK. Milan knows her. Oh, by the way," Zion said, almost forgetting, "Tomika called and said she'll be by tomorrow to pick Milan up."

"She's coming to get Milan?" Bruh said sarcastically, "We'll talk about that when I come back. But listen, baby, I need to run out. I got business to take care of."

"Where are you going?"

"Didn't we talk about this, Z? "

"I know." Zion took a deep breath, "I love you."

"Not as much as I love you," Bruh responded.

Bruh was uneasy about just coming home from prison and having to take care of business and movin' unnecessary work so soon. He looked at Zion and thought about how he needed to give up the game.

Feeling his vibe, Zion said, "Tell me that this is the last run."

"I'ma try baby."

"No, put it on your word." Tears filled her eyes, "This is it."

"Ai'ight,baby. This is the last run. After this, we done."

"True story?"

"True story."

"OK, now." Zion tried to smile, "Don't make me have to ride or die."

"You so corny, Ma." Bruh chuckled at Zion's silliness.

Sef blew the horn and Bruh kissed Zion good-bye on the lips. "Wait up for me Ma." And then he left.

Once he was in Sef's car, Bruh looked at Sef and said, "Where the nigga at?"

"He should be on his way home." Sef insisted, "If we get there now, we can beat him inside."

"Let's ride . . ."

<u>*Part 99: 'Movin' Work*</u>

THERE IS A CERTAIN SOUND that the 'hood makes when you steppin' to it. It's a sound that places you in a trance and the trance leads you to think about why you're so caught up in the street. Where and when did it start; how and why? Do you keep the beat of the street in your heart, until the valves pump a hip-hop rhythm that whispers, ". . . Don't stop . . . we got the beat that'll make your body rock . . ." These were Bruh's thoughts as he and Sef zoomed through the streets of Newark.

As soon as Bruh left, Zion started to panic. Her head spun and butterflies roamed the pit of her stomach, fluttering up acid as she thought of never seeing the man she loved, ever again. Zion's breath felt stifled as she started feeling that she needed to see Bruh again in order to breathe.

She placed her hand on her abdomen and

started bending over in cramp-like pain. She wiped her brow and stood up straight. She rushed around the house unintentionally waking her sleeping cousin in Seven's room.

"Zion," her cousin said, running out of Seven's room, "What's wrong?"

"Bruh!" Zion cried, "I just know its something. I gotta get to him. He needs me, I know he does!"

"Z, calm down!" her cousin yelled, "Please!"

"OK," Zion said, monitoring her tone, "I'ma calm down."

Half asleep, Milan stumbled out of Seven's room, wiped her eyes and asked, "Zion, where's my daddy?"

Desperately trying to hold tears back, Zion assured Milan that everything was OK and to go back to sleep.

Once Zion calmed her house down, she paced the floor and then she decided that she couldn't take it anymore. She ran up the stairs to her top dresser drawer and grabbed her .380, loaded it, ran back down the stairs, and left.

Zion jumped in her car, revved the engine, and took off. On her way to find Bruh she started thinking about how Tomika had confided in her that Haas was stealing Bruh's shit and taking it to Atlanta, setting up shop.

Zion felt in her heart that it was only a matter

of time before Bruh found out. When he came into the house today with the look that said he knew it all, she knew it was on.

* * * *

Sef and Bruh pulled up in front Haas' building and parked the car.Thoughts of prison crossed Bruh's mind as he prepared himself to check Haas the fuck out. He was growing tired of being in this same spot repeatedly; Bruh started thinking about his life and getting out the game.

Visions of his old prison cell crept into his mind as he thought about the blinding strips of the sun making their way from the small adjacent window and sneaking behind the forbidden walls to leave a trail of light on the concrete floor.

Bruh grabbed his gun and pulled his black ski mask over his face. He remembered that his prison cell felt like an asthmatic bubble with rounded bars, steel bunks, and a toilet floating in space; a bubble that forced his eyes to bulge out as he pictured himself rolling and handling his shit better the next time.Knowing fo' sho' that the game ain't nothin' to be fucked with, especially when the grand prizes are jail, Heaven, or Hell.

This was a vision that Bruh could not take. The déjà vu of being locked away ached Bruh's mind as he thought about being closed off from the world and placed into a population of unwanted human invasions.

These were all Bruh's thoughts as he and Sef popped the lock on Haas' apartment door and cased the place. They sat down on the floor, behind the door, with the guns pointed waiting for Haas to stroll in.

Bruh's thoughts began to drift once more as he thought about what he was going to do with Sef. He knew he couldn't have Sef get out of line again. But at the same time he loved Sef, like a brothah . . .

Fuck it, Bruh thought to himself, *I'ma take my daughter, my girl, her shorty and chill. Just chill and get some shit in perspective, like how I'ma change my heart, still get this money and be legal when doin' the shit.*

Bruh shook his thoughts as the doorknob turned and Haas walked in with Tomika behind him. Bruh looked Tomika dead in her face and then glared at Haas. He walked over to Tomika with his gun still pointed and slapped the shit out of her. "Stupid bitch!" Even with his ski mask on Tomika knew who he was.

After slapping Tomika, Bruh looked at Haas and prepared to pop the glock. He walked closer to Haas as Tomika, who was holding her face, moved further away; she didn't know if Bruh was coming for her again or not. Sef pointed his gun at Tomika and said, "Slow the fuck down!"

Bruh kept his glock pointed at Haas but started

speaking to Tomika. "I can't believe this shit! This the nigga you been fuckin'?" Bruh's ski mask stuck to his face as sweat oozed from his temples. He snatched the mask off and continued to shout at Tomika while looking at Haas. "You couldn't get a ma'fucker on the same level as me, or some ole other outside nigga? You fuck somebody in my ma'fuckin' camp and one that ain't no good? A nigga beneath me? One that don't even take care of his son?"

Bruh pressed the gun against Haas' forehead and tightened his grip on the trigger, "Say your prayers." Bruh stared Haas in the eyes.

"Bruh, please," Hass begged. "I swear to God, I won't do it no more!"

"Is that your prayer?" Bruh asked.

"Maybe, maybe not." Sef pointed his gun toward Bruh, with his finger against the trigger. "But it may as well be your prayer, because you checkin' outta here ma'fucker!"

"What?" Bruh asked in disbelief. His heart started pounding as he whipped his neck around, to look Sef in the eye.

"You really thought you could come home and steal my shit?" Sef demanded, "I been workin' this ma'fuckin' pavement, beatin' these streets, keepin' niggas in line. Me! And you just get outta prison and think you can come and step back at the top? Fuck no!"

Bruh thought that some shit might jump off with Sef; he just never expected it to be like this . . . or right now. Bruh was too caught off guard to quickly change his position. His glock was still pointed toward Haas, although he was looking at Sef.

Sef was staring at Bruh with beams of sweat oozing from his temples and blinding him. He blinked and caught Haas moving in toward Bruh in an attempt to snatch the gun.

In a split second, Sef turned toward Haas and blasted him. Tomika started screaming as Haas' blood splattered all over her.

Anticipating Sef shooting Haas, Bruh quickly turned his gun on Sef and said, "I can't believe this man!" Sweat poured down Bruh's temples. "How did we get here? You s'pose to be my nigga, my boy, the one holding it down for me, and you turn on me?"

"Fuck all that. This was my shit! I held the blocks down; I stepped up in the game. Me, Sef. Not you. This is it, ma'fucker. Repent for some shit, because you done!"

A bullet grazed the air and penetrated the side of Sef's head. A strip of moonlight lit up the floor as Zion flew from behind the door with her .380 in her hand. Her index finger was still on the trigger. "Rest in peace ma'fucker!"

Bruh could only stare at Zion in confusion, he

was too stunned to say anything.

Tears drowned Zion's vision as she continued to point the gun. Bruh placed his gun next to his feet, held his arms out, and said to Zion, "Come here, baby."

Hearing Bruh's voice and knowing that he was still alive Zion relaxed her stomach. She never noticed Tomika crying, screaming, and practically drowning in Haas' blood, with Sef now laying at her feet.

Still in shock and crying, Zion slowly lowered her gun, walked toward Bruh, and fell into his embrace. She tried to speak but her lips began to tremble uncontrollably.

"Don't say nothin'," Bruh whispered while wiping Zion's tears away, "It's all a part of the game baby . . . and sometimes the last run is an unexpected one."

DS

Fair Exchange, No Robberies

Acknowledgements

First and foremost let me begin my acknowledgements by giving praise unto the most high, my heavenly Father, God. He is my creator, my friend and my protector. It is through him that I'm beginning to find out who I truly am and my purpose here upon this earth.It is such a blessing just to be in his presence. I thank him for my life, my gift and most of all the Blood of Jesus.

Kaden, Mommy's baby, I'll never be able to put my love for you into words. Always know that Mommy loves you and no matter how big you get you'll always be my baby boy.

Los, my fiancé, my friend, who in the world ever thought that it would be us!? Like you said it must be destiny. I love you because no matter what we're going through I know that you truly love me. It's kinda like one of my favorite singer sings, "Every moment hasn't been perfect but when it's perfect it feels like were the only two people that have something real." Wherever this road called life takes you, whether it's smooth or rough, I'm riding.I love you!

Mommy and Daddy, thanks for the love and nourishment. A special thanks to all of my Grandparents for that special love. Thanks to my sisters and brothers for holding me down. To all of my aunts, cousins, uncles and close friends thanks for all of the love and support.

Tu-Shonda Whitaker, my co-de. You are so talented and blessed. Keep doing your thing ma and let the haters hate.I have so much love for you. Thank you for all the advice whether it's professional or personal.

Thanks for the fifty phone calls a day and keeping me focused on my goals. I also look forward to many Oprah and Gail moments with you (smile).

Vickie Stringer...where do I begin? I don't care what the mad authors say, the haters say or what the gossipers say .You are such a beautiful person and you have been so wonderful to me. You are a super agent and a shrewd business woman. Thanks again for getting me that six-figure deal ma. You are a great friend and a fantastic big sister/role model. Thanks for placing that tiara on my head...I love that the haters hate it. They only mad 'cause I wear it so well. Vickie you know how we do...Love is Love and Real Recognize Real!

Nakia Murray thanks for the love and the realness. You are the best literary publicist in the game. You're the best because you love the art and you really care.

K. Elliot thanks for holding me down fam! Kwan Foye, thanks for always keeping it real. Kiesha Ervin, I see you ma *Chyna Black* is a good look. Ki Ki Swinson, its all love ma. Treasure E. Blue trust me it's love see you on the Harlem World tour.

Tanya Blount, I cherish and thank you for the friendship that we're building.

A special thanks to Mia, Tammy and the TCP staff for all your hard work on this and other projects.

Tu-shonda and TN, I truly enjoyed working with you. See you two chicks on the tour.

And to all the haters stay on your job...you're just MOTIVATION!!

Fair Exchange, No Robberies

Mmph...Mmph... Look at him up there, Lovi thought. *My baby is still fine as all hell. That navy Ralph Lauren suit fits him perfect. Still fly. Still got his swagger. That's exactly why all these hos is up in here hootin' and hollerin'. But that don't matter. As always, right now I'm the center of his attention. And it's been that way since the day we met.* Lovi smiled down at her exquisite two-and-a-half-carat engagement ring that Nicky had given her only days earlier. Staring at the blue streaks running through the magnificent solitaire put her in a trance, taking her back to the day they first met...

* * * * *

"Nigga, you need to quit playin' down there in ATL and come get some of this Winston Salem money!" Dough bragged to his longtime friend/business partner, Nicky. "I' m telling you, these fiends out here! Man, they buy dope like kids buy gum. And all these niggas is coppin' our work. They know they can step on that shit four or five times and it'll still make a fiend OD."

Nicky laughed at his friend's charisma. "Dough, I'm getting that guape in ATL, I don't know what the fuck you thought. Plus, I blend in down there. Up here, your flashy ass stick out like a nigga at a Klan rally."

"I know you're not calling me flashy and you just bought a yacht! Besides, I think the real reason you still down there is... you waiting and hoping your baby mother come home."

The subject of Mira, his baby's mother, was sensitive. And Dough's comment had struck a nerve. "Man, whatever, just open the door. It's hotter than hell out here."

They entered the house continuing to trade friendly insults. Nicky dropped his duffel bag in the middle of the foyer and pulled off his T-shirt revealing a gray wife beater. "Cut the air on. It's hotter in here than it is outside."

"It's broke."

"Broke?"

"Yeah, nigga. Stop complaining, go in the kitchen and help bust down some of that work before you leave. I gotta go take this bitch to get an abortion, man."

Nicky walked into the kitchen as Lovi was coming out. The sight of her statuesque body stopped him in his tracks. Her breasts were perfectly round and sat high on her chest. Looking at her ass, he had to tell his dick, *Stay down.* The girl's ass looked like she was half reindeer. *Dough got a winner,* he thought. *Her measurements must be 36-26-43.* The print of Lovi's round, hard nipples peeked through her thin white tank top. The super-short terrycloth *BeBe* shorts exposed her big milk chocolate thighs. Her skin glistened from a thin layer of perspiration. Her auburn hair was braided in eight thick cornrows that stopped at her shoulders. Nicky wondered what she looked like beneath the surgical mask that she was wore. All that he could see of her face were her beautiful charcoal colored eyes that sparkled like diamonds.

Whew, he's fine! Lovi thought as she stared at Nicky. He needed more than the word "fine" to describe him. He needed words like beautiful, amazing, or simply gorgeous. He looked like the average homeboy, but with classic good looks like Blair Underwood. *Where did he get that complexion? I've never seen such pretty shade of brown. Hmm, and that body...let me stop. Who is this nigga? Boy, I'm slippin'! He could be here to rob me.* She stopped admiring him and asked, "Who in the fuck are you?"

Nicky was caught off guard by her aggressive approach. The mouth didn't match the sparkly eyes or the heavenly body. Dough walked up and interjected. "L, this is my man Nicky. Don't you remember Nicky?"

"No, I don't. And where're the window air conditioners?"

"Umm..."

"Umm, what? I know your black ass didn't come back up in here without those damn AC's! It's not enough I drove the shit down here for you because the incompetent bitches you employ can't do their jobs without doing dumb shit to get arrested. I already cut your shit up in that flaming ass kitchen but I'm not bagging up your bundles in that blazing inferno."

"Come on, L, I forgot. I was rushing to get Nicky from the airport... and now I got to rush over here to take Rashida to the clinic."

"That's not my problem. Stop running up in hood rats raw and you wouldn't be making trips to the clinic. I don't understand why you can't give her the money and let one of her lil' chicken-head friends take her."

"'Cause I'm not getting tricked again. Don't get me wrong, I love my daughter. But Chloe's ass was supposed to take that money and get an abortion, not buy them damn Manolo Timbs."

Nicky wanted to know what this girl had on Dough that he let her get away with the cursing and smart comments. Usually Dough would smack fire out of any male or female if they came out of their mouth the wrong way. But he wasn't even getting upset or making her stop.

Dough walked past Lovi to the huge stainless steel refrigerator. "Chill, L. It's a *Wal-Mart* over there by the clinic. You'll be aight, Nicky boy is gonna help you till I get back." He grabbed a *Pepsi*, popped the tab open, and guzzled it down. After giving Nicky a pound he kissed Lovi on the cheek and headed for the front door. "I'll be back in 'bout two hours."

Lovi gave Nicky the once-over before walking back into the gourmet kitchen. She grabbed a surgical mask and tossed it to him. "Knock yaself out."

Nicky caught it one handed, *I hope this chick know she not going be talking that shit to me like she was talking to Dough.* He took a seat at the glass table, never taking his eyes off her. In the center of the table was a four-inch high, ten-wide, neat pile of heroin ground into powder form. It was off-white, almost gray in color.

Lovi sat down and emptied a box of tiny cellophane bags onto the table. Without saying a word she pulled two scales from a black jewelry box. They were shaped like sterling silver tiny spoons with skulls carved on the ends. She passed one to Nicky. Methodically Lovi picked up one baggie and rubbed it between her pointer finger and thumb to open it up. Using the spoon-shaped scale she scooped up a gram of heroine and emptied it into the baggie. After folding the bag down three times she pulled a strip of tape from the edge of the table, and sealed the bag shut.

Nicky watched her with a critical eye. "It's going to take all day doing it that way. Why don't you fill your bags until you got like fifty then go back and tape them?"

"I don't think I need your crash course in Bagging Dope 101. I've been doing it since I was thirteen."

"Sweetheart, I was just trying to help you out. You don't have to get all defensive."

"I wasn't."

"Then I hate to see you when you do."

Lovi cut her eyes at him. She reached over and pressed "play" on the CD player. The sounds of Anthony Hamilton filled the room. *I guess she wants me to shut up. I'ma keep fucking with her. She not my bitch, she could never be; her mouth is too damn slick. She must got Dough's ass whipped.* "I've always wondered about girls like you."

"What do you mean, girls like me?"

"Don't get me wrong, 'cause I'm from *the* ,hood. But you tough ass hood chicks, with your gun totin', weed smokin', I'm-holding-my-man-down mentality... y'all kill me. I mean, I'm glad my man got you here to hold him down. But if something happens to him, what happens to you?"

This motherfucker is working my nerves. Let me bust his shit real quick. "So you think you know me, huh? You think I'm one of Dough's little stupid hos that do anything he ask, for a pair of Air Max?"

"I mean, if the shoe fits," Nicky smirked.

Lovi removed the mask from her face to reveal full lips, a perfect chin and high chiseled cheekbones. *Now he's pissing me off.* Her anger caused her eyes to light up more. "Let me explain something to you my man." She softened her tone. "No, better yet, excuse me, sir. I happen to hold a bachelor's degree in pre-law from the University of North Carolina at Chapel Hill, where I also minored in history. Next semester I'll be attending law school at Columbia."

She was more beautiful than Nicky had ever imagined. "So now I get it. You're a little rich good girl looking for a thrill with a nigga from the 'hood."

"I'm not looking for shit. I do this 'cause it's family business. My mother sold dope, her mother sold coke, and her mother's mother bootlegged liquor when it was illegal. And I can assure you, if anything happens to my *brother*, I'll be able to hold my own."

"Ya brother?"

"Yes, ass. Dough is my brother."

She can't be. Nicky looked closer at Lovi. *It is her.* "Lovi? Little Lovi?"

"Yes."

"Damn, I swear I didn't know that was you. I haven't seen you since Dough sent you away to that all-girls school."

"Sorry, but I don't remember *you*."

"I'm Nicholas Belger. My family lived down the block from Dough's grandmom's house. You would always try to follow Dough and me around. You were only like six. Dough's grandmom would make you stay in the house."

Lovi looked at Nicky closely. Dough and all his friends were at least six years older than she. Knowing he had to be referring back to a time when she was six or seven, she forced herself to remember. She didn't want to remember. It meant remembering her mother being killed execution-style while she watched from her hiding space in her mother's closet. Lovi had blocked out most of her childhood memories, just to be rid of that one. Suddenly they all came rushing back: her trips to Dough's grandmother's house in Brooklyn, and Nicky's face as a child. Then an image of her Mother's body falling to the floor sneaked in. The white carpet soaked in blood. Lovi shut her eyes and squeezed them tight. *No...no...no, don't think about it. Please God, make them go away.*

"Lovi, are you okay?" Nicky asked as rose from his seat. He gave her a little nudge. "Can you hear me? Lovi, say something!" *God, I hope she not hav-*

ing a seizure and we got all this shit up in here.

Lovi opened her eyes and shook her head, literally shaking off the memories. "I'm OK." She got up to get a glass of water. Lovi's hips brushed against Nicky when she passed by. He felt the blood rush to his dick. *Look at those thighs; I know they're soft as hell. I really can't be having these types of thoughts - this is my man's little sister. I can't believe she grew up to be that beautiful and that body...God, that body...*

Lovi's voice brought Nicky back to reality. "I remember you now," she said as she leaned against the sink. After taking a swig of water she cleared her throat. "Didn't you turn out turn out to be one fine ass nigga? Far from the lil rusty nigga that used to get in trouble with Dough."

Her disposition was sexy as hell. Nicky couldn't even look at her any more with out risking an erection. Without taking his eyes off the dope that he was bagging Nicky told her, "Lovi, I know you're hot in here, 'cause I'm burning the fuck up. But could you please put on something else?"

"Why?"

"'Cause. I can't be looking at you with that little shit on and not think about you in *other* ways."

"What's wrong with that? I was thinking about you in *other* ways when I saw you."

Why did she have to go there? "You're Dough's little sister. I can't believe he let you walk around in that little shit. Back in the day he would've beat your ass."

"Well this ain't back in the day. I'm grown. *We're* grown." Lovi sat down and got back to work.

"I see you still like to take risks. Is that what got Jamie killed while I was locked up?"

"What?"

"I heard Jamie Smark got his self killed for fucking with Dough's little sister, after Dough had put out the word that nobody was to fuck with you."

"I'm not saying who killed him or if I know anything about it. Allegedly he was killed for his disrespect. It seems he didn't understand no meant *no*." Lovi sealed her comment with a sexy smirk.

"One thing that ain't changed about you is that smart ass mouth."

"Tell me about it." They both laughed which took the conversation into a friendlier atmosphere. Lovi continued to openly flirt with Nicky, bringing the sexual tension to a head. Nicky was hoping Dough would return soon before he yielded to the temptation called Lovi.

Six hours had passed and still no sign of Dough. They'd finished bagging and packaging the bundles of dope. Now there was nothing to take Nicky's attention away from Lovi. *I have to get out of here, man. Where the fuck is this nigga at?* He tried dialing Dough's number for the fifth time. "Yo, where you think your brother at? I'm not going to keep calling him like I'm a bitch."

"He probably over that girl house, petting her and shit, like he do after every abortion. I wish he would come the hell on. I'm starving'"

"Me too. Where's the car you drove down?"

"That's the car Dough is driving. His car is in the shop. He was supposed to pick up a rental this morning. You know what, there's a really good soul food restaurant around the corner. It looks like a juke joint. I mean, dancing and the whole nine in a little shack. But the food and drinks are great, not to mention it's in walking distance."

"I'm with that. Can I get some towels for the shower?"

"Use the bathroom down here in Dough's room. There are towels under the sink."

Nicky took a cold shower and tried to scrub off the lust he was feeling for Lovi. It was more than lust; he was infatuated with her. Her eyes, oh how he loved her eyes! The way she looked at him as if she were peering into his soul. Nicky turned off the water and stood in the shower for a few seconds before stepping out. He quickly dried his body and applied cocoa butter. He chose a plain gray T-shirt, baggy blue jean shorts, and a pair of gray *New Balances*. A flawless diamond earring in his left ear and a wide diamond bracelet served as his accessories for the evening. Once he slid his plastic Glock .9mm in his waistband, Nicky knew his outfit was complete.

"You ready?" Lovi hollered down to him.

"Yeah, I'm coming out now." Nicky walked out of the bedroom and shut the door behind him. He took one look at Lovi and the emotions that he'd tried to wash away in the shower came rushing back. *What is she trying to do to me?* Lovi had taken her cornrows out and her hair was wild and wavy. She wore clear *Chanel* gloss on her lips and sheer pink eye shadow and blush. Her clothes weren't anything spectacular. She wore a white tank top, light blue pair of *Paper Denim* capri jeans with a wide cuff and a hot pink belt with a huge rhinestone buckle. The shoes were another story. On her feet were the sexiest hot pink *Christian Louboutin* open-toed stilettos showing off her lovely French pedicure. The narrow four-inch heels stiffened her already defined mocha calves.

"You must like what you see," Lovi said seductively cutting her eyes at him.

Nicky wanted to tell her that he loved what he saw, but it wouldn't come out. Instead he reverted to the games that young schoolboys played when they had a crush. "I hope your big ass can walk in those shoes, 'cause I damn sure ain't carrying you."

"I doubt that you could if you had to...probably couldn't carry my thong."

I'll show you what I can do with your thong, Nicky thought with a devilish smile. Lovi walked over and lifted the cushion on the couch, revealing a small arsenal of firearms ranging from handguns to a sawed-off shotgun. Looking over at Nicky she asked, "Do you need something?"

"Nah, Ma, I'm good."

Lovi picked up compact chrome and black Ruger and placed it in her pink Bottega Veneta clutch.

*   *   *   *   *

Rigby's Place definitely qualified as a hole in the wall. It was a downtrodden box-shaped building in desperate need of a paint job. It appeared that much hadn't changed since the established date of 1966, which was hung proudly by the entrance. Inside it was dimly lit. Small square and round dining tables surrounded a makeshift dance floor. A slim rectangular table with DJ equipment was set up in the corner. A tall, lanky, light-skinned man with a grotesque face was spinning a mix of old and new school R&B and rap records. A few girls were on the dance floor doing their best booty bounce to crunk music, trying to capture the attention of the local ballers.

Nicky watched them with amusement as he ate his food. The girls did nothing for him. They all looked rough, like they had been around the block a few times. Plus, he could tell what kind of games they were playing. Lovi watched him as he watched the girls. "So *that's* what you like?"

"What?"

"I mean, you looking at them with a smile. All I get is a hateful glare."

"*Man*, come on. I'm smilin' 'cause they gamin' and they fuckin' jokes. This whole setup is a joke. But you wasn't lying about the food, it is bangin'."

Rigby's neared what had to be beyond capacity, as the one o'clock hour approached. Now the dance floor was filled with males and females grinding their bodies into one another. The fans that were strategically set up throughout the building did nothing but circulate hot air. Somehow the intense heat seemed to send a sexual charge through the club.

Sexuality oozed from Lovi's movements as she danced around in her chair, swaying side-to-side and rotating her tiny waist round and round. She was feeling the effects of the three Long Island Iced Teas she'd consumed during dinner. Nicky watched her. Wanted her. His mind was sober. He never drank in unfamiliar surroundings; just never knew when shit was going to pop off.

"Come on, I want to dance. I love this song." Lovi grabbed Nicky's arm and pulled him toward the dance floor.

"No. Stop. I don't *dance*." Nicky couldn't resist her. He protested yet he followed her onto the dance floor. They danced to Terror Squad's *Take You Home*. "Daddy, let me take you home," Lovi sang playfully, while rubbing her body into his. Feeling the gun in his waistband and joked, "Damn, I make you feel like that?"

Nicky let out a little laugh. "You really want to know how you make me feel?"

"As if you would tell me."

"I want you bad...but..."

"But what? And don't say nothing about me being Dough's little sister."

"That's exactly what I was about to say."

Lovi stopped dancing and placed her hands on her hips. "Let me put this in terms that you will understand. I want you, you want me. We both get what we want. Fair exchange...no robberies."

Suddenly the ugly DJ switched the record to "Drop Down." The crowd went crazy as they chanted along with Nelly, "Drop down, get your eagle on, girl."

"Oh hell no," Nicky stated firmly. "I'm not dancing to this shit. Let's go."

"No. I happen to like this song. You can have a seat, leave, do what you want to do. I have no issues with dancing alone." Lovi smiled and did a booty hop that would put Beyonce´ to shame.

Nicky sat down and watched her. With expert movement she rolled, gyrated, and jerked her body to the rhythm of the song. Following the song's instructions she dropped down low in those four-inch heels and popped her pelvis in and out. Lovi mouthed the words, "Sweat dripping all over my body," as she stared at Nicky. The suggestive dancing, looks, and the shoes had him gone.

Nicky wasn't so gone that he didn't notice the lustful stares that Lovi received from other niggas. They were drooling over her. Niggas who were dancing with other girls stopped dancing to watch her, so now the bitches were in full hater mode. Nicky peeped them rolling their eyes at Lovi and whispering. *Let me get her ass out of here before these hos get it twisted and start some shit.* He stood up and waived the waitress over to the table. The five-foot-nothing, busty waitress walked over to him switching the entire way. He handed her three twenty-dollar bills. "Keep the change."

That made her night, seeing that the check was only thirty dollars. She smiled at him, showing off two gold front teeth. "I like your style, cat daddy. Thanks"

"You got that, Ma." Nicky walked over and grabbed Lovi. "Come on, girl. Let's go before I fuck around and catch a case behind your ass."

"That's where you want to be? Behind *my* ass?"

* * * * *

"What you gonna do, playboy?" Lovi asked as she climbed the stairs. Nicky's eyes followed her plump ass as she walked. In the next few seconds, so did he. Nicky stood in the bedroom door and watched as she stripped down to her unmentionables. Nicky stepped inside the room, shut the door and locked it behind him. Walking over to Lovi he pulled off his shirt. He had a spectacular chest. It had been perfectly chiseled during a two-and-a-half-year bid.

They stood chest-to-chest. Slowly Nicky explored Lovi's body with his soft hands. Her body was equally soft. *Um, she feels so good.* He ran his hands over her back and down the contour of her waistline, squeezing it softly.

Lovi couldn't believe it was happening. Her legs were shaking like it was her first time. Her body quivered. With every touch of his hands she flinched.

Nicky palmed her ass and gave it a squeeze. *It is Charmin soft,* he laughed to himself. He continued to massage her backside as he stroked her left ear with soft wet licks from the tip of his tongue.

"Um," She moaned as her creamy liquid began to flow down and soak her thong.

Nicky ran his fingers through her hair and held her head steady. His soft warm tongue slid gracefully into her mouth before he pulled it out, then plunged it back in again. Nicky finally caught her tongue and sucked it gently. The kiss alone was *almost* enough to make her come.

Using one hand he unsnapped her bra and pulled it off. He slipped his right hand into her thong hand past her silky pussy hairs. He parted her vaginal lips with his middle finger and slowly traced the entrance of her hot throbbing middle. He wanted to know what the inside felt like. Gently he fingered her; it was so wet and tight and just around one finger! The feeling drove him crazy. *Now*, he *had* to give her hard cock...and sort the rest out later.

Nicky pulled Lovi's thong down over her wide hips and voluptuous thighs, past her wonderfully strong calves. She stepped out of it and kicked it aside with her cute toes. Lovi removed his gun, dropping it on the bed behind her. Then she unbuckled his belt and assisted him out of his shorts. He had a massive erection protruding from his navy Sean John boxers. The size and the hardness turned Lovi on more. "Now I really *know* how I make you feel," she laughed sexily.

Using his body, Nicky guided Lovi onto the queen-sized bed. He continued to kiss her passionately all over. He parted her thighs with his face and sucked her clit.

"Oh, God...oh, God. *Nicky!*" She shuddered. Nicky pushed her legs back until her knees were touching her bare breasts and dove into her tongue first. He licked and slurped her sweet juices. She tasted *so* good. Letting his tongue lead the way, he licked her with one long stroke and made his way back to her face.

Lovi was in heaven and she wanted Nicky to join her. She locked her legs around him and pushed him to the side, forcing him onto his back. She straddled him slightly and let the head of his dick graze her wetness. Closing her small hand around his long, thick hard dick, Lovi held it steady and slid onto it. "Umm..." she whimpered as she continued to ease him inside of her.

He closed his eyes as he moaned, "Hmm, Lovi...Damn Lovi." Her shit was so tight around his dick. Once she had every inch of him inside her she had the nerve to flex her inner muscles and squeezed his dick with her wet walls.

Lovi lifted her body so only his head remained inside of her. Slowly she eased back down, then up again, in a steady rhythm. It felt good to finally break her two-month drought. Gradually her strokes picked up and she tossed her head back and rode him like a wild buck.

Nicky opened his eyes and looked up at her. All sorts of thoughts ran through his head.

Beautiful.

Intelligent.

Sexy.

Ambitious.

Dough's little sister!

Then the images of Lovi crying on his shoulder at her mother's funeral crept into his head. Her long thick ponytails, her little shiny black patent leather shoes dangling from the front pew, and the heavy sobs that came from deep inside of her tiny body. Now, staring at her, she was no longer the sexy twenty-four-year-old beauty. She was little Lovi. *I can't do this. This is wrong.* Roughly Nicky pushed her aside and pulled out of her. He jumped up and pulled his boxers and shorts back on. He grabbed his shirt and shoes.

What tha hell? Lovi sat up, watching him in disbelief. "What tha fuck, *yo?*"

Nicky couldn't turn to face her. If he did, he would weaken and go back inside her, so he spoke with his back to her. "Look, Lovi. This should've never went this far. I can't do this. My bad." He unlocked the door and opened it.

Lovi leaped from the bed and slammed the door shut. "Hell no! You… you…you're not getting out of here that easy. What the fuck is it with you? You a fucking fag?"

"Lovi, don't play yourself." Nicky held onto the doorknob, looking straight ahead. "You just don't get it. And you *should* get it. You know the game and the rules. By doing what we just did I violated Dough and you."

"Here we go again. What the fuck man? Dough is not Scarface and you're not Manolo. Get over these bullshit street ethics."

"Ma, just let it go."

"*No!* You fucking let it go! Getting up between my legs ain't shit to you. You'll finish busting that nut with the next one." Lovi removed her hand from the door and walked back toward the bed.

Nicky grabbed her wrist. "You don't know me and it's not like that."

"Fuck you! You selfish bastard!" Lovi yelled at him and snatched her wrist out of his firm grip. Through gritted teeth she told him, "Just go... get the fuck out, you tease!"

"Lovi..."

She cut him off, "Don't say shit to me." She went into the bathroom and slammed the door.

Nicky pulled the bedroom door open and slid out. *What the fuck did I just do?*

* * * * *

My head is killing me, Lovi thought while slowly rolling out of bed. The three Long Island Iced Teas from the night before were now kicking her ass. She went into the bathroom and took a long, hot shower. At 9 a.m., the heat was already becoming unbearable. Lovi slipped into pair of yellow ter-rycloth *Juicy Couture* hot pants and the matching fitted tee. She pulled her wild hair back into a clip.

Just as she was about to walk out of the room, she noticed Nicky's gun on the bed. Scenes from the night before played out in her mind and made her headache worse. Lovi snatched the gun from the bed and proceeded out of the room.

Walking down the stairs she could hear Nicky and Dough laughing loudly. Four window unit air conditioner boxes were on the living room floor. Lovi entered the kitchen, to see Dough and Nicky eating from *Waffle House* Styrofoam containers. *Sorry ass niggas didn't even see if I wanted something.*

"You forgot this during your big exit." She placed the gun next to Nicky.

Nicky became a bit nervous, fearing that Lovi would try to put him on Broadway in front of Dough.

Lovi had no intention of doing such a thing. She looked over at her brother, and said, "And I'm glad to see you got your nose out that bitch's ass long enough to make sure I wanted some air or something to eat."

"Lovi, you know I couldn't just leave her afterwards."

"Fuck her! You knew it wasn't a car here, no fucking food and it was hot as all hell." Lovi opened a bottle of Aleve and poured three pills into the palm of her hand. She popped all three in her mouth and chased it down with a can of *Cherry Pepsi*. "Give me the keys to *my* rental car. I got somewhere to go."

"What time you coming back? I need to get Nicky to the airport."

"Fuck *him*! He can take a cab."

Slamming his fist on the table, Dough stood up and got in his sister's face. "I'm getting tired of your mouth. You better check that shit before I check it for you. And you know it ain't going to be nothing nice." His temple veins were pulsing on the side of his head. He tried to keep his composure with her.

Lovi didn't give a flying fuck about Dough's little outburst. Unlike most people around him, she didn't fear him one bit. But she decided to let the battle go. Rolling her eyes she stepped around him and snatched the keys off the table. She glared at both men with disgust as she stormed from the kitchen.

Dough took his seat and continued to try and calm himself. "Man, Nicky, I don't know what I'm going to do with her. Lately she been acting nuts. As much as I hate to say it, I think she need some dick. Her ass definitely need a man so she can stay the fuck out my personal B I."

"She probably trying to protect you, the same you've always did for her," Nicky told him.

"She needed my protection," Dough laughed. "Why don't you take her off my hands? Take her down to Atlanta and let her protect your ass."

Nicky searched Dough's face to see if there was any sincerity to what he was saying. Unsure of what he saw, he just joked back, "Nah man, I think she's more woman than I can handle."

*   *   *   *   *

Upstairs Lovi poured her belongings into her medium-sized, *Marc Jacobs* mint green leather handbag. She decided she would go and try out a local salon, one that one of Dough's girlfriend's recommended. She threw on her favorite *Ferragamo* shades and headed for the front door. When she opened it, two chicks stood before her. The short, thick one was about to press the bell. Lovi scanned their appearances. *Who the hell is these two bum ass bitches? They look a hot ghetto ass mess with them twisted ass weaves. And why this short bitch looking at me like I wasn't supposed to answer the door? Let her say something slick. I'ma light her little ass up.* "Can I help you?"

The short chick spoke up. "Yes, is this where Dough is? I'm looking for *Nicky.*"

Lovi caught an instant attitude. *Did this ho just put emphasis on Nicky?* "And who shall I say is here?"

"Huh?" The short girl questioned Lovi, dumb-founded.

"What is your name?"

"I'm Senica, and this is Octavia."

Lovi yelled back into the house, "Dough! Some ho name Senica is here for Nicky."

"Oh, *hell no!* Who the fuck this bitch think she is?" Senica stepped forward ready to thump on Lovi.

Lovi pulled her gun from her purse and stuck it in Senica's face. Senica froze where she stood.

"Back the fuck up, bitch. This is *my* house," Lovi smirked.

"L, what the hell is you doing? Get that gun out that girl face. They here to drive Nicky's work back to Atlanta." Dough said walking into the room with followed by Nicky.

Lovi lowered the gun never taking her attention away from Senica and Octavia.

They walked past her, visibly shaken, into the house. Senica wanted to know who this wannabe gangsta bitch was. She didn't give a damn if it was his wife. "Damn, Dough what kind of nut so security you keeping around? She probably ain't shit without that ratchet."

Lovi *was* ready to let the shit go. *I know this ho ain't trying to be slick.* "The burner is back in the bag. Now come taste me, if you think I'm sweet."

"Fall back, L."

"You too, Senica. This is Dough's little sister," Nicky interjected.

"I ain't mean no harm, honey," Senica said as

she hugged Nicky and placed a sloppy wet kiss on his lips. "But she started with me."

Lovi glared at Nicky. Who needed him? Was this the type of sluts he liked?

Nicky didn't even have to look at Lovi to feel the heat coming from her. When he did *look* at her, into those eyes that transfixed him, he saw that fire had replaced the sparkle. They also blazed with jealousy and hurt.

Lovi walked out of the door slamming it behind her. Nicky walked up on her as she got into a white rental Malibu. "*Lovi*, that shit wasn't necessary. I don't fuck with her like that." *Why am I explaining anything to her?*

As if she could read his mind Lovi answered, "Why the fuck are you telling me? Now I know who you'll finish getting *that nut* with!" She put the car in gear and merked off, leaving Nicky to eat her dust. It would be the last time they saw each other. At least for a while.

*   *   *   *   *

One re-up. No Lovi. Second re-up No Lovi. Third re-up... still *no* Lovi. It had been five weeks since that dreadfully hot day Nicky had laid eyes on her. And five weeks since her passion for him had nearly gotten Senica's face blown off. Every time Nicky went to meet Dough to replenish his heroine supply, he would inquire about her. He wanted to know where she was. How she was doing. Had she found a boyfriend to tame her aggressive-ass attitude? Dough would tell him in a jovial manner, "Damn, you sure do ask a lot of questions about Lovi. You wanna holler or something? I can hook y'all up."

Nicky never took Dough seriously when he said such things. Nicky would answer, "Damn, a nigga can't ask about her off of GP?"

Dough knew Nicky had a thing for his sister. Hell *any* nigga he brought around Lovi got a hard-on just by looking at her. Lovi was beautiful. Shit, the girl was bad as hell. She *was* the total package. If Nicky had been any other nigga, Dough wouldn't even allow him to speak her name. But when it came to Nicky, he didn't care and in his own subtle way, Dough was trying to let Nicky know that. Besides, he knew something had happened between the two of them. He could read their interactions on the last day that they saw each other. And the way they both wanted to be kept up to date on one another.

* * * * *

Where the fuck is Lovi? Dough wondered. *How the hell could she be late for something this important?* He looked down at the bulletin, after the next selection by the youth choir it would be time for his seven-month-old daughter, Carrington, to be christened. He looked down the pew. Everyone was in place: his father, Chloe, her parents and

Nicky. He had asked Lovi and Nicky to be Carrington's godparents, and Lovi was nowhere in sight. If she were to miss the ceremony he would never forgive her. Maybe he'd even choke her ass out.

Beads of perspiration broke out on Dough's forehead as the choir rose to sing. It was an unusually warm fall day for New York. Not to mention that the church was crowded and he was dressed in beautiful black two-piece wool blended suit. In less than ten minutes it would be time for Dough and his family to go to the altar, and the person that he would lay down his life for wasn't even there. His feelings were starting to hurt. Now the sweat was trickling down his forehead.

An usher, a tall slim lady with a peculiar-looking wig, appeared at the end of the pew next to Dough. He remembered her from when he entered the church before the service started. Looking up at her, he wondered why she was standing at his pew, then he that saw that she was directing someone to sit on his pew. Dough turned around and was able to exhale. *Finally.* It was Lovi and her boyfriend, NBA superstar Hakim Douglas. Lovi sat next to Dough and leaned to kiss him on the cheek. Dough embraced her and whispered in her ear, "Where in the fuck have you been?"

"Is your ass crazy?" Lovi whispered back. "How you gonna be saying the F-word in *church*?"

"Oh, so you can say 'ass', but I can't say fuck? Get the fuck outta here."

Lovi hit him with a sharp elbow in his side. "Stop cursing, boy!"

Hakim reached around Lovi to shake Dough's hand. "What up, man?"

"What up wit you, player?" Dough let his hand go. Both men sat back and tried to focus on the singing of the choir. Dough leaned over and whispered to Lovi, "What did you bring *him* for?"

"*Not now*, Dough."

Lovi knew that her brother hated Hakim. It wasn't that he hated Hakim the person. He hated Hakim the boyfriend, and not without good reason. Hakim was a certified ho. He fucked anything with a big butt and a smile. He did take a special interest in Lovi, though, but his shit was always front page. Every week he was fucking the hottest young actresses and singers then kicking them to the curb. The worst part of it for Dough was that the nigga was a megastar. If Hakim were to hurt Lovi, it would be hard for Dough to get at him without legal consequences.

By no means was Dough a saint. He personally understood a man's need to keep a woman on the side. Hell, he loved Chloe, but Rashida was his weakness. However, he would never let Rashida disrespect Chloe. That's *what* he really hated about Hakim! He was a disrespectful bastard. Just a year ago he had been engaged to one of the prettiest black girls in Hollywood, Zene Kirks. During their engagement he openly flaunted other women in public. Pictures of Hakim kissing and dancing intimately with other women were a permanent fixture in the tabloids. His behavior drove Zene insane. Literally. She tried to commit suicide after catching him having sex with her best friend and sitcom co-star, Bridgett Jeffries. A week later they mutually ended the engagement.

If it ever went down like that between Hakim and Lovi, Dough had already made up his mind that he would break both Hakim's legs. Quiet as kept, Lovi couldn't *stand* Hakim. He was a pretty boy. A rich kid. He grew up with an NBA star for a father. He had never known struggle, which made him naïve and a square in her eyes. This also meant that he could never be taken seriously as a long-term companion. But for the moment, he would do. Hakim was fine as all hell, 6'6" and a solid two hundred and thirty pounds. He had sharp, keen features which were covered by silky smooth skin that was darker than the richest chocolate. He wore his beautiful hair in cornrows that stopped at his shoulders. And his dick game was *serious*.

Hakim liked spending his free time with Lovi and taking her to exclusive events. Since they had been going out, he hadn't had sex with anyone else but her. For some reason, he treated her differently than he had treated all the others; probably, because she was one of the few who wasn't fascinated with him because he was a rich basketball star. Lovi refused to kiss his ass like the chicks to whom he had been accustomed. And most importantly, in true Lovi fashion, she said what ever the fuck she wanted to!

All through church service Nicky would glance at Lovi and glare coldly. *What the fuck is she doing here with him? It don't make a difference to me. But him? Everybody know he treat bitches like shit. She is looking good though...real good.* Lovi *was* doing the damn thing in a beige safari-inspired suit with brown trim by *Celine*. As always, her shoe game was on point. She sported a mean pair of brown gator pumps with three-inch heels. Her hair was flat-ironed bone straight, with a part in the middle. It flowed beautifully down her back. Lovi looked sleek and sophisticated, which only made Nicky want her more.

Lovi *wished* she were there with Nicky instead of Hakim. Hell, he was the reason that she had brought Hakim in the first place. It would have crushed her if she would have shown up by herself and Nicky was there with another chick. Now she felt stupid, this could've been her chance. She caught his glances and stares. If she hadn't brought stupid ass, Hakim with her, she *could've* been next to Nicky. Especially seeing that he was alone, and looking *damn* good in a brown single-breasted *Hugo Boss* suit. Together they would be perfect, they complemented each other's style.

* * * * *

After the service, Hakim had to leave immediately to attend a team meeting. Since Dough's car was full Lovi decided to hail a cab, go home, and pick up her car. Nicky saw her on the corner and pulled over. The tint on his white BMW 745i was so dark she didn't know that it was Nicky until he rolled the window down. "Yo, ma, you need a ride?"

On the inside Lovi was beaming. But on the exterior she was cool, calm, and collected. "Yeah, I just need to go to my place so I can get my car."

"I'm going to the dinner. You can ride with me if you want."

"Alright."

The wonderful smell of Nicky's Aqua Di Gio cologne filled the inside of his car. Lovi savored the sweet, sexy smell. She watched Nicky from the corner of her eye. *I hate him. Why is he doing this to me? He looks good as shit and he knows it. Over there singing that stupid ass Jaheim song. I wish he would just shut the fuck up. What in the hell do he know about putting a woman first?*

"What's on your mind?" Nicky interrupted her train of thought.

"Nothing. Why?"

"You seemed to be some where else."

"I'm just tired. I had a long night."

"I *bet*."

"What in the hell does that mean?"

Nicky ignored her "Can I ask you a question?"

"What?"

"Why you fucking with *him*?"

"Who? Hakim?"

"Yeah."

"Hold up," Lovi said, rolling her neck. "Who the fuck are you to question me? You had your chance. You blew it. So don't ever feel comfortable questioning me about any nigga I'm with. As a matter of fact pull over at the light so I can get a cab."

"I'm not pulling shit over. Your mouth is ridiculous. I just asked you a simple question and you spazzin' out."

"Well it's none of your fucking business." Lovi turned her head and smiled out the window. *Let me find out he jealous.*

Nicky stared her as they sat at the red light on 116th and Pleasant Avenue. He was feeling her. *I should give her a chance. Nah, fuck her, she too hardheaded anyway.* They rode down the FDR without saying a word to each other. Once they arrived at the Water Club, they avoided each other the entire time. When it was time to leave, Lovi had a car service waiting to ensure that she wouldn't have to take another ride with Nicky.

* * * * *

The constant ringing of Lovi's house phone was disturbing the most comfortable sleep that she'd had since the beginning of her midterms. She tried hard to ignore it but every time the answering machine would pick up, the caller would hang up and call right back. "The *fuck, man?*" Lovi screamed yanking off her black silk sleeping mask as she jumped out of bed. *"Hello?"*

"You have a collect call from, Dough, an inmate at the Forsythe county jail. To accept charges press one..."

Lovi pressed one immediately. She was familiar with her brother's trips to jail for petty shit, never for the real shit. She simply asked, "Who do I need to send the bail money to?"

"I need you to come down here. I don't have a bail." Dough's voice was void of all emotions.

"Why don't you have a bail?"

"My charge is murder one."

Lovi damn near passed out when she heard the words *murder one.* This couldn't be happening. She couldn't afford to lose Dough to a life sentence in some prison. He was all the family that she had left. "I'm on the next flight."

After a quick shower, she threw on a sky blue velour Juicy sweat suit. She placed a few important items in her Gucci backpack and practically ran out of the house. Once downstairs she hailed a cab and headed straight to LaGuardia Airport.

*   *   *   *   *

Three hours later Lovi sat on a metal stool peering at her brother through a glass partition, holding the phone to her ear. "So, who are they alleging that you killed?"

"Some kid named Jeff."

"Who is that? Or who was he?"

This was the part that Dough didn't want to tell her. His brown skin became a shade lighter. He broke eye contact with Lovi and looked around as if he were searching for the right words. "He was... he was Rashida's boyfriend."

"I thought that her boyfriend was in prison."

"He got out like a month ago."

Never trusting phones or the visiting booths, Lovi mouthed to him, "Did you merk him?"

Dough told her yes with a simple head nod. Tears stung the back of Lovi's eyes. She blinked furiously to fight them back. "So what's the story? Why do they think you did it?"

"Rashida told them."

"She *what*? I'm going to stomp a hole in that bitch."

"Lovi, it wasn't like that."

"What you mean, *it wasn't like that*? Don't tell me you all soft for that ho!"

"Nah just let me explain." Dough inhaled. "I get a call from Rashida two days ago. I hadn't talked to her since earlier that day when we left the abortion clinic."

"You took her to get *another* abortion? What is that, like, number six?"

"Yeah," Dough said with a little shame in his voice. "Anyway, that night she called me crying. Jeff had found the papers from the clinic while she was asleep. The papers showed that she was two-and-a-half months pregnant. So, naturally he kirked the fuck out and beat her out of her sleep. He'd been hearing shit about her and me while he was locked up. He told her that he was going to find me and do me in."

Lovi knew her brother too well. He didn't have to finish the story. She knew in the game he was always on the offensive team. "So how did it get back to that bitch?"

"One of her nosy-ass neighbors told the cops that it was Jeff who beat the shit out of her. So you know when them faggots brought her in, they was telling her how she could be charged with accessory or conspiracy. You know how the faggot ass jakes is; they hit her with the game."

"What other evidence do they have?"

"Nothing, man. No gun, no witnesses. Just her word."

"Nigga, you gonna beat this shit. And don't worry; I'll take care of Rashida."

Dough shook his head vigorously. "Chill, Lovi, I need you to handle something real important for me."

"Like what?"

"I got thirty pair of gray Air Force Ones packed and ready to go. I need you take them to Nicky down in ATL. You have to get them there tomorrow, by 3 p.m. He don't even know I'm locked up. The car is in the garage at your house. It's packed and ready to go. Get my Palm Pilot out of the glove compartment. The directions are in there."

She looked at her brother and smiled. "You know I'll hold the family business down until you hit the bricks, my nigga." She balled her fist and held it up to the glass. Dough did the same. The siblings exchanged a pound through the glass and told each other, "Lovi you my nigga." She hung up the phone and walked away so she wouldn't have to watch Dough being escorted away by the officer.

*   *   *   *   *

When Lovi left the jail she was open. She had to make sure that her appearance was on point before Nicky laid eyes on her. That meant an impromptu trip to the hair salon; and, of course, a pit stop in Charlotte on her way to Atlanta, to cop something fly to wear from *Nordstrom's*. But first, Rashida's snitching ass had to be dealt with.

* * * * *

Grief consumed Rashida's petite body. Her brown skin was battered with bruises. And her usually immaculate short haircut was a complete mess. She was also racked with physical pain and guilt. Not only that, she was forced to deal with it all by her lonesome. Jeff had been her boyfriend since the seventh grade and now he was gone. His mother, Cassandra, surely let Rashida know that she wasn't welcomed to grieve with the family. The day before she'd gone to Cassandra's house to seek comfort and solace. Instead, Cassandra met her at the door with over-cooked rage.

Cassandra couldn't believe that Rashida had the nerves to show her face at her home. In front of everybody she completely flipped out on her, screaming, "Get the hell away from my house, you slut! You should be ashamed to even show your face around here. It's all your fault that my baby is dead. You and that low life New York nigga. I don't want to ever see you again! And don't even dream of showing up at the funeral."

Rashida couldn't believe that this was the woman that she once lived with and called Mama. "But Miss Cassandra..."

Rashida's cousin, Felicia, wrapped her arm

around Rashida pulling her away, "Come on girl, let's go. You don't need this."

Jeff's best friend, Kyle, and a few other guys cut them off as they were leaving the yard. Kyle got right in Rashida's face and did all the talking. "The next time you talk to that northern nigga, you better let him know its money on his head. And I suggest you watch your own back."

The two girls stepped around Kyle and got into the car. He stared at them coldly until the car was out of sight. If looks could kill their car would have exploded.

Now Rashida wished that she hadn't told the police anything. Then, no one would have a clue about Dough's involvement. Hell, she couldn't even be sure if Dough really killed Jeff. He didn't tell her, she just assumed it that Dough had done it. She sat on the couch smoking a blunt, wishing that she could turn back the hands of time. *Why didn't I just burn them fucking clinic papers?*

Her thoughts were interrupted by a knock on the door. Remembering that she'd ordered a pizza, Rashida grabbed her purse and ran to the door. When she opened it, a hard right to her chin greeted her and knocked her to the floor.

Lovi stepped inside and slammed the door behind her. Rashida struggled to get up. Lovi kicked her in her chest and sent her back down. She bent down and kneed Rashida in the neck, pinning her to the floor. "I've never liked you. I don't know what my brother ever saw in your wack ass. You bum bitch! I swear on everything I love, you gonna correct this shit or I'll body your little ass."

Lovi threw a business card in Rashida's face. "That's your lawyer's card; you have a meeting with him tomorrow morning at nine. If you're late, I'm gonna come back here and beat the wheels off your punk ass. From now on, you don't speak to 5-0 unless he is present. And you're going to recant your statement. I don't give a fuck if you have to tell the cops you killed that motherfucker. Do you understand me?"

Rashida attempted to nod yes, which was hard considering that she had a grown woman's knee crushing her throat. Lovi stood to her feet. Rashida gasped for air, crying and coughing uncontrollably. Out of sheer spite, Lovi turned and stomped her in her stomach. "Next time bitch, find something softer to play with."

*   *   *   *   *

The next day, following the directions from Dough's Palm Pilot, Lovi drove to an auto body shop in Norcross, Georgia, right outside of Atlanta. A tall metal fence surrounded the entire building. Lovi pulled up to the locked entrance and tooted her horn three times. Butterflies flipped-flopped in her stomach as she waited for someone to open the fence. On the ride down she had been more nervous about seeing Nicky than she was about the thirty kilos of heroin stashed throughout the car.

About two minutes later a short, stocky, dark-skinned, bald man in a heavily oil-stained blue mechanics uniform walked over to the gate. When he saw her behind the wheel he stopped short and pulled out his Nextel phone. Lovi could tell that he was radioing someone on the inside of the shop. A few seconds passed. Then the man himself, Nicky, emerged from the shop and he was looking damn good. He was wearing lavender *Polo* button up, crisp blue jeans, and fresh gray *Prada* sneakers.

Nicky's heart fluttered a little when he saw Lovi behind the wheel. He yelled over to the man, "Open it up Moe. She's straight."

Once through the gate Lovi was directed to drive the car into the shop. As soon as she stepped out of the car and the garage door was down the workers began to take the car apart. They pulled bricks from every nook and cranny imaginable. Nicky led Lovi to his office and tried hard not to openly drool over how good she looked. Her hair was in a bounty of long curls. She was wearing a gorgeous form-fitting turquoise

open turtleneck sweater from *Cache*; a pair of super-tight *7 Jeans* that made her ass look nuts;

and, as always, she was rocking' the meanest shoes, a pair of turquoise and lime green snake-skin *Roberto Cavalli* stiletto boots.

Every man in the shop stared at Lovi's ass and gave one another a look of approval as Nicky led her into the office. "So where my man at?" Nicky asked, shutting the door to the plush office. It was way too plush to be in an auto body shop.

"He's locked up," Lovi answered, as she sat in an ultra soft baby blue leather chair across from Nicky's big oak desk.

"So why didn't you bail him out?"

"'Cause, he doesn't have a bail. They got him on a murder one charge."

"For who?"

"Rashida's boyfriend, Jeff."

"I thought that nigga was in prison."

"Me too." Lovi went on to tell him the story that Dough had told her. Once she finished the story, Nicky didn't hold back on how he felt. "I swear to God, man, Dough get real stupid when it comes to these hos. I been told him that bitch wasn't shit. Even our lil' young nigga out in Winston told him that her man was straight killer, and that she wasn't worth the drama. Dough didn't have a choice but to eighty-six that man. All this trouble for a bitch that ain't even *his*. And you telling me her birdbrain ass is the one who dropped the dime on him?"

"True story."

"You should've whipped her ass 'til she couldn't walk."

Lovi dropped her head, "Nicky, I could've did that girl real dirty. But we already know she's a straight snitch. She not built for this game. I just want my brother out. I can't lose him to the system for crazy years. He's all I got." Tears snuck into her eyes again. This time one escaped, streaking down the right side of her face. Her hurt and frustration only made her more attractive in Nicky's eyes. Today she was humble and oh so vulnerable.

They talked for another hour or so. Not about anything in particular, just shooting the breeze. Nicky looked down at his watch and realized that they needed to be bringing the conversation to an end. "Lovi, I'm getting ready to make some moves with that work you brought me. I got some people coming by to pick it up. I mean, you know what time it is."

"Oh so what you're saying is, you want me to leave."

"Yeah, you know I can't have you here in the middle of this shit. In case something goes wrong."

"I understand. Did they put the car back together yet?"

"Nah, you not taking that car back, anyway. What you got planned for the day?"

"I'm going to check into a hotel. Then maybe go over to Lenox Mall, do some light shopping, catch a movie, get something to eat and call it a night."

"Here, take my car." Nicky handed her a set of keys. "I'ma give you the directions to my house. You can stay there tonight. By the time you leave the mall I should be on my way home. Just in case I'm not there, I'll tell my maid to let you in."

"Your *maid*? Damn, you doin' it way big."

*   *   *   *   *

Oh this nigga is really doing it. No fucking wonder he needs a maid. This shit must be at least twelve to fourteen thousand square feet, easy, Lovi thought as she drove up to the beautiful white brick and cobblestone house that Nicky called home. She pulled his Suburban into the circular driveway, wondering if she should put it in one of his four garages that sat on the side of the house. She quickly figured out to her that she wouldn't be able to park it in any of the garage spaces since all four already held a big boy toy. In the first garage sat the 745 that she'd seen in New York. In the second, a black Hummer; in the third a gray Phantom; and in the fourth sat a BMW motorcycle and a Harley.

Damn, Mr. Nicky, I had no idea you played like

this. Lovi closed the garage doors and left the truck parked in front of the first garage door. She retrieved a massive amount of shopping bags from the rear of the truck. *So much for light shopping*, she thought as she struggled to carry the bags to the front door in one trip.

When Lovi got inside the mall she blacked out and spent nearly $25,000. She used Dough's incarceration as excuse to shop. Anytime she was in a crisis or felt bad, she used shopping to get her through it. It felt very good to spend five thousand in *Adrienne Vittadini*. The seven thousand the she'd dropped in *Vuitton* made her feel great. And the ten she splurged in *Neiman* made her feel like a new woman.

Nicky's maid, Maggie, was clad in a gray and white maid's uniform. She was a tall, big-boned, light-skinned lady with a big, pretty smile. She appeared to be in her late forties, but she was actually fifty-nine. Maggie swung the door open and made a small fuss over Lovi in her warm southern drawl. "Come on in, chile. I was expecting you hours ago."

"Sorry. I stayed at the mall longer than I planned."

"Let me help you with some of them bags."

"That's okay. I got it."

Now this one I might like, Maggie thought, as she gave Lovi an approving once-over. The other girls that had been privileged enough to visit Nicky's home were too stuck on themselves. They took the whole idea of Maggie being the maid a little too far. Usually they tried to dump all their bags on her, or expected her to clean up behind every mess that they made. But Lovi *could* definitely be a keeper.

The inside of the house was more amazing than the outside. The formal living room was decorated in warm and welcoming browns, beiges, and dark oranges. It was so warm and inviting. A huge black and white photo of a little girl with big-bright eyes hung over the mantle. She appeared to be about five years old. Lovi took it all in as Maggie led her up to one of the three luxurious guest rooms. Like the rest of the house, the room was magnificent. A king-sized brown leather bed sat in the middle of the soft beige carpeted floor. It was covered in a soft beige duvet and loaded with beige and brown leather pillows. *This shit look better than mines. Who would have thought that Nicky had such good taste?*

"Nicholas will be home shortly. And dinner will be served promptly at nine-thirty," Maggie said as she turned to leave the room. She turned back and told Lovi, "Proper attire is preferred for dinner."

* * * * *

Nicky let out a huge laugh when Lovi entered the formal dining room donning a silk black halter, black slacks, and a pair of silver *Casedi* pumps. He wasn't laughing because she didn't look good. Trust, every time he laid his eyes on her he thought that she looked better than the time before. Nicky was laughing because he knew Maggie had hit her with the *preferred attire* line. And that she'd fallen for it.

"And why aren't you dressed, *Nicky?*" Lovi noticed that he was wearing same clothes from earlier that day.

Nicky was still laughing, "I see Maggie got you with that dress-up shit."

"Oh, I see. Joke's on me."

"Not really. She be dead serious about that dressing-for-dinner shit. She's one of those old school housekeepers. She used to working for those real rich white people. You know, the kind that dress up for dinner every night. She always telling me I should dress proper; I just don't pay her no mind though."

"Oh well, the food looks and smells delicious," she said examining the chicken marsala, mushrooms, and potatoes. Lovi said her grace quietly before digging in. Nicky could feel her energy and tell that she was feeling better. They barely spoke a word while they ate. Once she finished with her food Lovi asked, "Where is Maggie?"

Nicky was enjoying a slice of carrot cake, "She's gone home."

"If I don't see her before I leave, tell her I said the food was really good."

After dessert, they retreated to the informal living room. Lovi kicked off her pumps and plopped down on the soft blue suede sectional. Nicky hit a few buttons and a flat screen monitor slid from the ceiling. The movie "Casino" was playing. He went behind the bar, which was stocked better than most small clubs. "You want a drink?"

"Yeah, *Hypnotiq* and *Gray Goose* mixed." Lovi peered at the screen. "Casino" was one of her favorite movies. Nicky handed her the drink and sat on the other end of the sectional. Lovi watched him as he took two shots of *Hennessy*. "So, who is the beautiful little girl in the pictures?"

"That's my daughter, Genesis."

"Wow, that's a beautiful name. Where is she now, with her mother?"

"Nah, she lives with my sister in Mt. Vernon." There was an unmistakable bitterness in his voice.

"Where is her mother? If you don't mind me asking."

"A few months after Genesis was born she left. Said she was going to Hollywood to pursue her career." Nicky took another shot of *Hennessy* "She said the baby and me were holding her back. Haven't seen her since. She sends Genesis birthday and Christmas gifts every year, but she has never been back to see her."

"Damn, Nicky. I'm sorry."

He liked the way that she said his name more than that he loved her empathetic side. "It's nothing to be sorry about. So what are you going to do while Dough is locked up?"

"What can I do, but hold the family business down?" Lovi smirked.

Nicky didn't find her answer amusing. He had fallen head over heels for her and he wanted her out of the game. She was in too deep. At that level of the game, only a few made it out with their freedom or their lives.

Nicky's cold stare made Lovi uneasy. "Why are you looking at me like that?"

"Lovi, the family business is what got your mother killed."

"Nicky, why did you have to go there?" Lovi tossed her drink back and tried to not to think of her mother's brutal murder.

"I went there because I don't want to lose you to the *family business.*"

"Didn't know you had me to lose me." She got up and stood over him. "Did you run it by Dough first?"

"I think we're pretty much to the point where that doesn't matter anymore. We're both getting what we want. You said it best: *fair exchange, no robberies.*"

"I felt like I got robbed the last time we were in this position," Lovi said in a sexy voice.

"I think it'll be different this time."

"Is that so?" Lovi bent down and kissed him. Her cool wet tongue danced in his mouth. Nicky dug his hand into her mass of curls and pressed the back of her head closer, forcing her to kiss him deeper. She broke his strong embrace and traced his right ear with the tip of her tongue. That was Nicky's spot, too. His erection grew even harder. Lovi moved her wet tongue from his ear to his neck, where she used her full lips to suck and her tongue to tickle.

"Hmm," Nicky moaned. He squeezed her body tight as she continued to explore his neck with her mouth. Lovi ripped his shirt open, popping every last button off. Using one hand she held his wife beater up and began giving his chest and abdomen the same treatment she'd given his neck. With her other hand she unbuckled his pants and pulled out what she wanted: that dick - and it was hard as steel.

Lovi dropped to her knees and positioned herself between Nicky's legs. She placed her hand around his shaft and looked up him. "I don't want to get robbed this time." She touched the tip of her tongue to the base of his dick and ran the flat part of it right up his main vein.

"Ooh." Relaxing, Nicky laid his head back and

closed his eyes while Lovi wrapped her glossy lips around his swollen head. She flicked her tongue back and forth across the sensitive area and squeezed it tightly between her tongue and the roof of her mouth. Lovi sucked it as if she were trying to get to the center of a Blow Pop.

Inch by inch, Lovi held her jaws tightly and took a little more of him into her mouth. Her head game was oh so serious. Seeing her head bobbing up and down was turning Nicky on more and more. "Oh shit, *Lovi*," he moaned as she took his dick deep into her throat, tightening her jaw muscles even more. Nicky ran both of his hands through her curls and pressed her head closer which only made her suck harder and faster. He couldn't take it anymore. Lovi's head was so good; she was making him feel like a bitch. He released her head. "Lovi stop. Baby, please, stop. I don't wanna come yet."

Lovi stopped and slowly slid her mouth off of his dick. With a little giggle she told him, "But I want you to come now...then again and again." She tongue kissed the tip of his dick.

"Stop playing, Lovi." Nicky stood and lifted her to her feet. Pulling her close, he wrapped his arms around her waist and held her snug. Now it was his turn to give her well-deserved kisses all over her face and neck. Without missing a beat he untied her halter. It fell around her waist to reveal her full, perky, bare breasts. Her nipples were erect and longing to be touched. Nicky did them one better and took them into his mouth, sucking and licking.

Lovi felt trickles of liquid forming inside of her walls. Nicky continued kissing her as he unbuttoned her pants. He reached down to remove her panties and was slightly shocked and very turned on when he realized that she wasn't wearing any. "Were you looking for something?" Her voice was dripped with lust.

"No panties, huh? You only made it easier for me to find. Come on, let's go upstairs."

"No. Let's finish this one right here." Lovi helped Nicky remove his clothes. She squatted to the floor before she laid flat on her back pulling him down with her. Tired of the foreplay and ready for the main course, she spread-eagled. They locked eyes and hers said, "Put it in now." Nicky slid in nice and easy with the help of the wet cream lining from her inside. "Damn, Ma, you're so wet."

"Only for you."

Nicky pressed Lovi's legs all the way back until her knees touched her shoulders. The way he had her positioned when he stroked in and out, his shaft rubbed against her clit. That shit sent chills up her spine. With her legs pinned down she couldn't really throw it back at him the way that she wanted to. Lovi kicked her legs, freeing them from his embrace, and began freaking him back.

The warm, creamy tightness wrapped around Nicky's rock-hard dick was bananas. "Lovi, your pussy feels so good. It's so wet." The more she rolled it around and around the better it felt and the harder it was for him to maintain. Lovi pulled out her favorite trick and began flexing her pussy muscles.

Nicky had to get her back under control. He rose to his knees. Holding onto her thighs, he raised Lovi's ass up off the floor. He pushed her thighs back and forth sliding her up and down his dick. Lovi couldn't take it. "Oh, baby. Oh...oh...that feels so good. Hmm...hmm..." She moaned over and over. Her eyes began to tear up as she became wetter and wetter. Then hot liquid exploded inside her rushing down her walls. "*Nicky*, I'm comin'. Oh...oh...oh. Oh my God."

Her voice was way too sexy. Her hot come on his dick felt too good. Nicky let go of her legs lowering his body onto hers, thrusting in and out of her, faster and faster. His long and hard strokes made Lovi's back rub against the carpet. It burned like hell; she was sure she'd have carpet burn marks in the morning, but she didn't care. In a twisted way the burning sensation on her back made the sex even better.

"*Lovi!*" Nicky cried out. He shook and jerked as he busted a long, hard nut, shooting a hot wad up in her. He collapsed on top of her and panted until he was able to catch his breath. "Lovi that was so good. Ma you just don't know how great it felt to get that off."

"Trust me; I know exactly how you feel. I do know one thing…"

"What's that?"

"I'm ready to take it into the bedroom now."

Nicky led her to his master bedroom, where they made love. Then fucked. Then made love again. Then fucked again and again until the sun came up. And when it did, Nicky called Maggie and gave her the day off. He rolled over and went back to sleep, only to be awoken by Lovi riding him. After they climaxed she fell into a deep sleep. Nicky slipped on his pajama pants and went downstairs, where he cooked her a big breakfast.

The food gave them the energy to start all over again. And when they started they didn't stop until they'd christened almost every room in his house.

* * * * *

With each passing week Nicky and Lovi fell harder and harder for one another. They'd both known that they really liked one another, but they had no idea their feelings for each other would grow so deep, so quickly. Nicky made Lovi feel like she could just go and fly away. He showed her more love than even he knew he had to give.

Nicky's love tamed her. It brought out Lovi's affectionate, lovable side, and she gave it all to him. When they were apart, they spent hours on the phone like two teenage lovers getting to know each other better. They were learning each other's innermost thoughts, loves, and fears.

On most Thursdays after her last class, Lovi was on a plane to Winston-Salem to visit Dough. Against Nicky's wishes she was still taking care of Dough's business. She was meeting his connect, serving his customers, and collecting all debts that were owed to him. This was the only thing Lovi and Nicky seemed to argue about. The same argument usually took place every Sunday morning when she arrived in Atlanta to see him after leaving Winston-Salem. Most of the time Lovi would arrive at Nicky's house and go straight to sleep. On one particular Sunday, the week before Christmas to be exact, the argument got more heated than any of the previous ones.

They were lying in bed talking after making love. Lovi was wrapped snugly in Nicky's arms with her back to his chest. "I'm so tired," she complained. "I could stay just like this - here with you, for days on end."

"You wouldn't be so tired if you weren't trying to go to law school in New York and be the Queen Pin of North Carolina."

Lovi sighed. "I thought that this was a closed

discussion."

"Why? Just because you want it to be closed? Nah, ma, it don't work that way. I told you before; you're doing too much. I can take care of Dough's shit and give you his money to hold until he gets out. We have the same connect, anyway."

"But *not* the same customers," Lovi argued as she turned to face Nicky.

"Are you trying to say I would steal his customers? Don't play me, Lovi. You know that I'm not a grimy nigga." He got out of the bed and started putting on his clothes.

"Trust me; I know you're not *that* type of nigga. And it's not about that. *I* promised *my* brother that *I* would hold him down."

"And how are you going to that if your ass is locked up? Or what happens when one of these nigga's decides to test you? Then who's going to hold Dough down?"

"You acting like the same shit can't happen to you."

"This is a man's game, Lovi. And most of them can't play without fouling out!"

"You're talking about a game that I've been playing for most of my life. And no one ever told me I was required to have a dick in order to play." She got up as well and began to dress.

"Lovi, we're together now. Let me take care of

you while you concentrate on school."

"Oh, now I see what this is really about. I intimidate you, don't I?"

"Hell no!"

"Well, what is it, then? Why won't you let me do me? And when Dough gets around this bullshit case, I'm out."

"Lovi, anything could happen between now and then."

Why is he putting the pressure on? I can't deal with this shit. "Look, Nicky, I don't know about this. Maybe this relationship isn't a good idea after all." Lovi grabbed all of her things. "I'm going back to Winston. I can't deal with all this right now."

Nicky blocked her exit. "I'm not through talking to you."

"What do we need to keep talking about the same shit for? You're never going to see it my way and I'm definitely never going to see it yours!" Lovi stepped around him to walk out the bedroom door.

"Lovi, if you leave... don't come back."

She stopped in her tracks. She thought about it. *Slow down, L, think this through. Don't let your ego mess this one up, too. Nah, fuck that. No nigga will ever run me.* Lovi turned to Nicky, "If that's the way you feel then *fuck* you, too."

Nicky just stood and watched her walking out of his house, and possibly out of his life. He let her walk away without not so much as a "wait a minute." He wasn't about to beg her. *Fuck her. That's her problem now. Too used to niggas catering to her. Maybe she was right. Maybe the relationship was a* mistake.

*   *   *   *   *

After making sure Dough's customers were squared away for the remainder of the week, Lovi flew back to New York on Christmas Eve. She spent Christmas day alone in her apartment. Dough's father had invited her to spend the holiday with him and his family. She declined the offer, telling him that she had other plans. She loved Dough's father as if he were her biological but as she grew older, his fatherly love only reminded her of the fact that she would never know her real father.

Lovi also had the option of spending Christmas with the wonderful Hakim. Hell, he had called her only fifty times in a row that day. She almost picked up the phone and invited him over, but that was out of the question. She didn't want to give him one ray of hope that there could ever be anything between them again. Once Lovi ended things with him, Hakim damn near stalked her. He bought her gifts, sent her flowers, and popped up at her house unannounced. She couldn't fathom how Mr. Ladies' Man all of a sudden only wanted her. After giving it some thought, Lovi came to the conclusion that *it must have been my snap back,* referring to the power of pussy. *It has caused a few to turn into stalkers.* She wanted to be with Nicky on Christmas and no substitute named Hakim would do for the occasion.

It was a miserable day for her. Hell, the last four days without Nicky were miserable. She'd picked up the phone a hundred times to call him, only to hang up before even dialing his number. To hell with him, he hadn't even called to see if she was alive. Lovi spent the whole day alone reading *Game Over.* She was finished by eight-thirty that night. Lovi contemplated calling some of her old home girls to see if they wanted to party, but she wasn't in the mood. She drank eggnog and called it night. Besides, she needed to wake early in the morning and go down to Fifth Avenue to return the gifts she'd purchased for Nicky.

* * * * *

Nicky was happy to have his entire family at his house for Christmas, but it didn't feel right without Lovi. He sat watching his daughter Genesis play with her new toys. She ran over to him. "Daddy, are those my gifts, too?" She pointed to a dozen gift-wrapped boxes.

Nicky stared at them for a moment. "Nah, those are for Daddy's other special girl. Go play with Auntie Michelle. Daddy gotta go do something." He went up to his bedroom and sat on the edge of the bed. He stared at the phone for a few seconds before picking it up.

Probably ain't nobody but fucking Hakim whining, Lovi thought as she got up to answer the phone. A smile spread across her face when she read the Caller ID. "Hello?"

"What you doing?"

Her heart dropped just from hearing his voice. "Nothing. Getting dressed," she lied.

"Where you going?"

"To a party, at the *Cherry Lounge.*"

"That's what's up. How's your Christmas been so far?"

"It's been great," she said, lying again. "How has yours been?"

"It was OK. I mean my parents, my daughter, and my sisters all came down. That's the best part about it, getting to spend time with them." *It would be better if you were here*, he thought.

"That's nice."

"I was calling to invite you to my yacht party on New Year's Eve, down at the pier."

"In New York?"

"Yeah, but I forgot which pier it is. My nigga set all that up. It ain't nothing big though, just some of my peoples. It starts at 9 p.m. It will probably end a little after twelve…"

"I'll come."

"Aight. I'll call you and give you the pier number later in the week."

"Talk to you later then." Lovi hung up the phone and danced around like a little kid. She was so happy just to have heard from him.

* * * * *

Nicky looked around the deck of his yacht. His New Year's Eve party was hit. So much money in air, you could smell it. Everyone on board was dripping with ice, their bodies wrapped in the hottest furs. He watched his friends and business associates, who were accompanied by their wives, girlfriends, or mistresses. All enjoyed bottles of champagne, made toast, and posed for pictures as the midnight hour steadily approached. Nicky tried to enjoy himself, but he was sick that Lovi didn't show up. He couldn't understand why she didn't come. She had even called earlier that day to get the pier number.

I'm not fucking with her ass no more. That's my word. She be on that bullshit. I can't be going through these emotions over a bitch, its bad for business. Nicky stared out at the water. He felt a light tap on his shoulder. Turning around he came face to face with Lovi. She looked so beautiful in a floor-length gray and black chinchilla with the hood covering her head. Her make-up was flawless. Looking at her made him forget the promise he'd just made to himself seconds earlier.

They stood and stared at each other for what seemed like an eternity. Nicky pulled her in and hugged her tight. "I'm glad you finally decided to show."

"Fifty stick-up kids couldn't have kept me away tonight. I've missed you so much this last week," Lovi said with her head still on his chest.

"I missed you too. With your mean ass," he laughed.

Suddenly loud fireworks lit up the New York skyline. The clock had struck midnight. Nicky kissed Lovi deeply before they turned to watch the light show. Lovi was elated and right where she wanted to be, bringing in 2005 with Nicky. She was really superstitious. Since childhood she believed that whatever she was doing when the New Year came in, was what she would be doing for the rest of the year.

After the fireworks, all the party guests exited the boat and headed for various clubs throughout the city. Standing side by side at the top of the steps Nicky and Lovi waved goodbye to everyone. She turned to him, "I have a surprise for you." Lovi unbuttoned her coat and held it open for Nicky to see. She wasn't wearing anything but shimmering body lotion and gray thigh-high leather boots.

"Yo, you is nuts, B." Nicky slid his arms inside

her coat wrapping them around her naked body. "But that's what I love about you."

"What else do *you* love about me?" Lovi slipped her hands inside his pants and rubbed his rock-hard dick.

"Let's go downstairs and I'll show you."

Lovi turned and dropped her coat to give Nicky the most wonderful view of her ass jiggling as she walked down into the cabin. He was stuck in the same position, smiling and watching her. Once he was able to move he picked up her coat and rushed down to the cabin thinking, *I'm gonna tear her ass up tonight.*

Once inside the huge cabin area Nicky threw both of their coats onto the living room couch. When he walked into the bedroom, Lovi was standing in the middle of the room with her hands on her bare hips and her head cocked to the side. A sexy smile crossed her face. "Come get some...if you ain't scared."

Nicky turned her around, bent her over the foot of the bed, and slid right in. Lovi's pussy was dripping wet and oh so hot. It was wetter than he'd remembered. "Hmm...hmm," he moaned biting down on his lower lip while grinding in and out of her slowly. "Ma, what you trying to do to me?"

"Only what you let me," Lovi panted in a high pitched voice while running from him a little.

"Stop running, unless its *you* that's scared."

"I ain't running. And I ain't never scared," she replied, rolling and grinding, throwing it back at him hard.

Nicky shut all that down when he covered her neck and back with wet licks and kisses as continued to stroke her crazy. Lovi's body went limp, tears streamed from her eyes, and her legs shook uncontrollably as her wet cream came gushing out. "Oh baby, I love you," she screamed.

"I love you, too. Do me a favor."

"What, baby?"

"Let me put it in your ass, ma." Nicky made it sound so sexy.

"Huh?" *Did he say what I think he said?* The half bottle of Cristal she'd just consumed had her just drunk enough to do it. "Only if you're gentle."

Nicky lubricated Lovi's anus with her own juices. He massaged and fingered her throbbing pussy as he put the head of his dick in her anal hole. "*Ah, shit,*" they groaned in unison. Nicky groaned from pure pleasure; it felt like he was fucking a virgin. Lovi's groaning came from the intense pain and pressure. But once he got it all the way in, her pain quickly turned to pleasure. It almost felt better in her ass than it did in her pussy. Within the first three strokes she was having another orgasm. *I wish I knew it felt like this a long time ago,* Lovi thought.

Around ten strokes of her tight ass was all that

Nicky could take before he was nuttin' everywhere. Afterwards, they collapsed onto the bed cuddling, kissing, and sharing pillow talk. "I want you to go somewhere with me tomorrow. But you have to wear clothes."

"Shut up, stupid." Lovi giggled. "Where are we going?"

"It's a surprise."

*   *   *   *   *

Nicky's surprise was New Year's Day dinner at his parents' house. They made Lovi feel like family. She absolutely loved his mother, Gladys. She was an eloquent and sophisticated woman with skin was the color of tar that was smoother than a baby's bottom. Her long, natural, jet-black hair was pulled back neatly into a nice, thick ball at the nape of her neck.

Nicky's father, Bruce, was a classic gentleman. He was a throwback to the old school gangsta. It wasn't hard to tell who Nicky had gotten his style from. Bruce was fair-skinned with thick wooly hair. Lovi now understood that Nicky's beautiful brown skin was a perfect blend of his parents' complexions.

When Gladys laid eyes on Lovi the first thing she told her was, "You are the spitting image of your mother when she was your age."

"You knew my mother?"

"I sure did. And I knew you when you were a baby." She grabbed Lovi and hugged her. They both felt an instant bond. Nicky's sisters, Bren and Leah, welcomed Lovi to the family with open arms. But his daughter, Genesis loved her. She followed Lovi around all day and sat next to her at dinner. Lovi didn't mind. Genesis was the sweetest six-year-old child she'd ever met.

During dinner Nicky stood up. "I'm glad Lovi was able to share this occasion with us. I'm glad y'all had a chance to meet the love of my life and witness this special moment." Nicky knelt down on one knee next to Lovi's chair. Lovi, along with all the women in the room, became teary-eyed.

Lovi was so nervous; *I know he is not about to propose!* Nicky pulled a black ring box from his pocket. *Oh my God, he is!* Two tears streaked her face. Never in a million years had she imagined that *anyone* would propose to her. Nicky looked her in the eye, "Lovi, will you marry me?"

Her bright smiled turned into a light giggle. She nodded her head nervously. "Yes, baby, yes I will."

He opened the box displaying a gorgeous two-and-a-half-carat princess cut solitaire, set in platinum. Lovi couldn't keep her left hand from shaking as he placed it on her finger.

"I love you so much," Nicky told her as he kissed her on the mouth.

"I love you more."

Everyone clapped and crowded around them to get a glimpse of the ring. The newly engaged couple hung around for another hour before heading back to Lovi's house. It was going to be a long night. They had a lot to celebrate.

* * * * *

Two days later Nicky and Lovi were back in Winston-Salem waiting excitedly outside the jail for Dough. His case had been dismissed due to a lack of evidence since Rashida had recanted her statement and disappeared. Lovi had so much to be happy for. Her brother was coming home and she would soon be Mrs. Nicholas Belger. How sweet was that?

When Dough finally emerged from the courthouse she jumped on him hugging him tight. "I'm so glad you're out, Dough."

"You glad? Nigga, I thought I wasn't ever getting out! I guess I should be thanking you for that."

"Why?" Lovi tried to act like she didn't have a clue.

"Whatever you said or did to Rashida must've worked."

"That's small potatoes. Let's talk about that later."

"Damn, can I at least give my man here some

dap?" Nicky interrupted the sibling moment.

"Yeah, baby, go ahead."

"*Baby?*" Dough questioned looking back and forth between them.

"I'll let you two have a moment. I'm gonna get back get in the car. It's getting too chilly for me."

The two men shared a pound and a quick embrace. "Damn, nigga I'm glad you got around this bullshit," Nicky stated. "I would've went crazy if they threw football numbers at you behind that broke down-hoe."

"My nigga, I done went crazy and came back sitting in that motherfucker. I'm glad to be out. But what's up with you and my sister?"

"I asked her to marry me."

"Get the fuck out of here," Dough laughed.

"I'm serious. We've been kicking it for almost three months now. I know you said you don't want niggas fucking with her, but I do love her and..."

Dough cut him off. "I never said that *you* couldn't fuck with Lovi. That was for them other niggas. I know you're a good nigga and you'll take care of her. I'm happy y'all together. There isn't another nigga alive I would rather see her with."

"That's love, my nigga."

"All the time. Now let's go get some food. A nigga is starving."

Fair Exchange, No Robberies

* * * * *

Kyle sat in the Expedition receiving the best head from his college chick. His groove was disturbed by the constant ringing of his cell phone. "Hold up a sec, shorty. Let me answer this one." He flipped the cell phone open. "What up, Swerve?"

"Yo, you ain't never gon' believe who just walked out of the courthouse."

"Who?"

"That nigga Dough."

"Ain't no way in hell that nigga out. You don't get no bail on murder one."

"The nigga is out. I'm sitting here looking at the nigga."

"Aight stay with that punk mother fucker. See where he goes."

* * * * *

Sitting in Copeland's with Dough and Nicky felt just right to Lovi. She felt secure, a feeling that had been absent the entire time Dough was locked up. With Nicky in her life she'd finally found happiness. On the inside she was beaming as they ate, conversed, joked, and laughed for hours. "Aight, I know y'all are enjoying my company and shit," Dough joked, "but a nigga need a shower and bitch so I can bust this nut."

Lovi rolled her eyes. "You need to wait 'til you

get up top and see your baby moms. Fucking with these outside hos is what almost had you're ass locked up for life."

"You know it's just jokes, sis." Dough smiled and winked at Nicky.

Nicky gave Lovi's shoulders a little squeeze. "Let my man live ma. You know…"

Lovi cut her eyes at him and he stopped talking. Dough busted out laughing. "I know my lil' sis ain't got you wrapped like that. Y'all niggas is funny, B. Let me go take a piss then we can get outta here."

"Nicky, don't encourage him."

He hushed her complaint with a big kiss, which she happily returned. Nicky pulled back and told her, "I love you and no matter what happens, don't ever forget that."

"I won't. Just keep reminding me and remember I love you more." Lovi kissed him again.

"Man, y'all cut that shit out," Dough said returning to the table.

"Jealous?" Lovi joked.

Dough looked at his sister like she was out of her mind. "Quit talking out your neck, girl. Come on, let's go."

Nicky threw the money for the bill and tip on the table as they got up to leave. Dough walked a few feet ahead of them as they exited the restaurant. He was looking down at his cell phone, scrolling through the phonebook. When he stepped onto the concrete right outside the glass doors, an old black Cutlass pulled up and the dark tinted windows slowly rolled down.

Dough looked up just in time to see the barrel of a sawed-off shotgun sticking out of the passenger-side window. He was fucked. He didn't have a burner and he was out in the open with nowhere to hide. His only concern now was keeping Lovi out of harm's way. He turned and screamed, "Nicky! Get Lovi down!"

Those were Dough's last words as the bullets ripped a massive hole in his back. Amazingly, he was still standing. A tear fell from his right eye and blood ran from his the corners of his mouth. For a few seconds he was frozen in time, his eyes locked with Lovi's. She was paralyzed as she stared back into his. In a shrilling voice she screamed out, *"Doooough!"* As his body fell to the ground.

The masked assailant stepped out of the car and walked towards Dough. Nicky shoved her back into the restaurant and grabbed her purse. "Stay here, Lovi."

Heated that he'd left his own gun in the car's stash box, Nicky ripped opened her oversized Gucci bag and stuck his hand in. Just like he thought, she was packing as usual. He pulled the 9-mm luger from her bag.

The masked man pumped another shot into Dough's lifeless body. Nicky let off five shots back-to-back as he stepped out of the restaurant, hitting the man once in the right side of his chest and once in the shoulder. Unable to hold onto his gun the man turned to run back to car. Nicky shot him again, this time hitting him in the thigh. The assailant fell to the ground. The back door of the Cutlass flew open and Kyle jumped out, gripping a Glock .45. He shot at Nicky but the first bullet missed his head by inches. The second one slammed into Nicky's heart. He died instantly.

Kyle went over to the masked man who was barely holding onto life, and dragged his body back to the car. Lovi crawled to the door and peeked out after the gunshots had stopped. The hostess, who was hiding behind a wall like most of the staff and customers, tried to stop her. "Miss, don't go out there. Wait for the police."

Lovi was oblivious to her words. Her heart dropped and felt like it was trying to come out of her stomach when she saw Nicky dead only inches from Dough's lifeless body. The words to one of her favorite Jay-Z songs ran through her head: *This can't be love, this can't be life, it's gotta be more, this can't be us.* Tears for her brother and the love of her life flowed from her eyes. She looked up and saw Kyle putting the man's body in the backseat. Her heart turned to ice as she crawled past Dough's body and over to Nicky's.

Lovi pried the gun from his hands. She kissed his bloody lips and whispered in his ear, "Don't worry baby. Them niggas is gonna pay." From her low position over Nicky's body she aimed and fired at Kyle. The bullet hit him square in the ass. He fell on top of the masked man's body in the back seat. "I'm hit!" Kyle yelled.

"Who the fuck is still shooting?" Swerve asked from the driver's seat.

"I don't know nigga. Get the fuck outta here."

Swerve pressed down on the gas and drove away. Lovi got up and ran towards the back of the car as it sped off. She let off wild rapid shots. A bullet shattered the rear window of the car. Swerve ducked down. Kyle yelled, "Who in the fuck?"

Swerve sat up and caught a glimpse of Lovi in the rearview mirror. "It's that bitch that was with them."

Lovi could hear the approaching sirens as she walked over to Dough's body and collapsed on top of him. She hugged him and cried like a baby. "I didn't get 'em this time. But I'll get 'em, baby boy. I put that on Mommy, I'll get 'em, starting with that slut Rashida." She kissed his forehead and laid his body flat. She made her way over to Nicky. She lifted his head and cradled it in her lap. Her off-white leather pants, and jacket were stained with Dough's and Nicky's blood.

Lovi's tears dripped upon Nicky's face as she

tried to talk. She gasped for air. She traced his hairline with her fingertips. "We said fair exchange, no robberies. Remember that, baby. Now I feel like...like I've been robbed. I'll never know what we could've been. I've been robbed of your love. I've been robbed of a chance to be the wife that you deserved, to take care of you and have your child." She looked over at Dough. "My niece and your daughter have been robbed of their fathers, the same way I was robbed of my mother. I couldn't do anything about that. But I promise you on Genesis's life, I will slay those niggas that robbed you and Dough of your lives." Lovi kissed Nicky's lips and laid her face on his. "Remember, I love you more."

*   *   *   *   *

"I don't want to sit with you! You're not my mommy. I want to sit with Lovi!" Genesis screamed as she clung to Lovi's skirt, bringing Lovi back from her trip down memory lane. She looked up and saw Mira, who was embarrassed that her daughter was making such a scene in the middle of Nicky's funeral. Gladys cut her red eyes at Mira. "Let the child be. I'll let you see her later."

Let me? I'm her fucking mother, Mira thought. She didn't dare say it aloud. She rolled her eyes at Lovi and simply walked to the back of the church and took a seat. *The nerve of some hos! I should've tripped her,* Lovi thought. She looked down the front pew and saw the funeral director talking to

Gladys and Bruce. She noticed they were both shaking their heads. She watched as he came towards her and Nicky's sisters. "We're about to close the coffin. We would like to give you a chance to view Nicholas once more."

Leah and Bren couldn't go back, but Lovi needed to. She needed one last conversation. She walked to the casket. The front of her black suit was stained with brown spots from where her tears had streaked her brown foundation. It now looked much like the one she had worn to Dough's funeral the day before. The church was filled beyond capacity. All the females' loud cries were now silenced as everyone watched Lovi. She bent down and whispered, "Baby, I'm going to miss you so much. I don't even know how to go on without you, Nicky. I wish I could just hold you one more time. Thanks for loving me. No man will ever take your place in my life. I promise to look after Genesis and I'll visit you as often as I can. Rest in peace; I have to go now, baby." She kissed his lips, "I love you more."

Throughout the service the only thing on her mind was the day that she would return to Winston-Salem. And on that day, every person that contributed to Dough and Nicky's death would die a cruel slow death. That's only fair, *right?*

TB

Rollin' Dice

Acknowledgements

First and foremost I have to Praise the Lord for my Blessings and for always giving me strength when I feel weak. I love you and I thank you Jesus!

Tiana, it's just me and you against the world. Mommy loves you!!!

To my family and few real friends that love me, support me and have my back no matter what, I love and thank you all.

VS, I want to thank you for the pep talks, your patience, support and for helping me get to this point...you're a real Jerry Maguire. Remember that movie? "Show me the money!" I love you for not only wanting the best for yourself but for your writers as well. Thank you so much!

Tammy, Benzo, Kevin, Mia and the rest of the TCP staff, thanks for always being such a big help when I'm in need.

My editor Maxine, thank you!

To my fellow TCP Authors...keep creating those bangers. I wish each every one of you guys much Happiness and lots of Success.

Much love to all the readers out there. Whether you love it or you hate it, I still thank you for your support.

And last but not least, I thank all the bookstores and street vendors for their support!!!!

Much love,

T. N. Baker

Rollin' Dice

"Whose pussy is this?"

"It's yours, Daddy!" Enychi would answer in a soft, seductive tone as she slowly rotated her hips and the walls of her wet pussy would squeeze tightly around my dick, causing me to bust all up in it every time. That's right. The pussy was mine, indeed. Enychi was my wifey for real, and when you talk about a nigga being so gone, I was him. Shortly after meeting her, I moved her into to my crib instantly and locked it down.

When I first met her, I knew I had to have her, so pursuing her was the easy part. Although Enychi damn sure gave me a run for my money by playing hard to get, eventually I succeeded. But shit was all good 'cause I'm that dude that's always up for a challenge and I knew I wasn't gonna stop until I made her mines. Word.

Shorty had it going on.

She was beautiful in every sense of the word. Smooth Hershey-colored skin, shoulder-length hair, chinky eyes, sexy lips and a body that'll make a nigga wanna spend all his dough on her.

I know because I did. I paid for her education, her hair, her nails and kept her wardrobe up with the latest fashion. Whatever she needed, I got it for her. It couldn't be no other way.

She was mine; she represented me. I ain't give a fuck. In fact, I looked at Shorty as more like an investment, not just some knucklehead chick with no direction. She had goals in life.

Enychi wanted to be one of the hottest designers in the fashion industry, so most of her time was spent focusing on school and keeping up with the latest trends. I supported her 100%. Besides, as fast as she could spend my dough, I made it back shooting dice on the block with the fellas.

Yeah, besides Enychi, that dice shit was a weakness. A nigga loved to get his gamble on and I was damn good at it, too. Fucking with them dice games until all times of the night was my hustle. Talking greasy and taking niggas' money was what I did. Catz hated to see me hit the block 'cause if they ain't already have a game going, they knew I was 'gon get it started and empty out pockets.

I'd start the bank off at no less than a thousand and by the end of the night, the stakes would always grow as high as 7 Gs. On the streets that was a considerable amount of paper being tossed around. Niggas couldn't fuck with me. My luck was crazy. I'm not saying I ain't lose every now and then, but that shit was rare—ya heard...

That is, until this nigga we called Pretty Tone - 'cause he a light-skinned, gray-eyed, long-braided, good-haired ma'fucka - came around and threw a monkey wrench in a nigga's game! Tone was an old-school nigga. Thirty-something years old with a rap sheet from back in the day that was crazy. Niggas knew not to be fooled by his pretty boy looks 'cause dude was still gangsta. After serving ten years state time for murder, it's alleged that when he came home he killed his cousin for not honoring the code of the streets.

Supposedly his cousin ratted him out for a murder they both took part in.

He wasn't stupid, though. Serving his time wisely, he took advantage of all the educational programs available, back when they existed. By the time he came home, he'd started his own business. Tone would come through the block every now and again, flashing a wad of cash and talking a shit load of trash. He'd make a nigga so mad that you couldn't help but gamble your last dollar, hoping to roll trips, just to shut his ass the fuck up and take his money along with the victory.

I was one of them and as much as I wanted to,

I couldn't front on the nigga because he was the truth. He had to be 'cause he was the only nigga out there, besides me, who could roll dice and take a nigga out his game, using my same strategy.

At first shit was cool 'cause like I said before, I was always up for a challenge.

But damn, who knew this nigga was out to do me dirty like that...I didn't even see it coming, but later on neither did he! It's been six months and two days since Tone rolled them trips, but I remember it like it was yesterday.

It was a Saturday morning and I woke up to my dick in Eynchi's mouth as she blessed me with some of her toe-curling head. Babygirl definitely had the skills to make a nigga weak at the knees. And I must say, what a way to start the day. After she finished sucking the early morning load of man milk out of me, I glanced at the clock. It read 10:45 a.m. I got up out of bed and headed for the shower. I was meeting up with a few of the homies to get an afternoon game of dice going.

By the time I finished washing my ass, Enychi had breakfast waiting for me – grits, cheese eggs, turkey bacon and some French toast. Honey went all out. She damn sure knew how to take care a nigga and I loved her for that.

"Wasuan, I need five hundred to pay my car note today," Enychi said.

"Oh, so that's why you woke a nigga up like

that this morning," I said, referring to her super head job.

"No, I just felt like taking care of my man, that's all."

"Oh, is that what it was?" I laughed, fucking around with her like I always did.

"Of course, that's what it is." She flashed me a devilish grin.

"Yeah a'ight," I said, wearing a crazy Kool-Aid smile. "Good answer."

Yeah, babygirl's morning sweet talk won a nigga over. "A'ight, Ma. I'ma have that for you later. Just meet me on the block—a'ight? I'm meeting up with the fellas at about twelve to get my shit off. I might even have a little more than that for you, if niggas come out to play.

"Here, blow on these for me for extra luck," I said, referring to my lucky iced-out set of dice that hung low from my chain. Enychi nodded her head as she walked up to me and gently blew on 'em.

"Ain't no stopping me now," I said as I play-fully popped her on that nice soft ass of hers and sat down to the kitchen table to get my eat on.

"Wasuan, what happens if one day you get in too deep and lose all of our money?"

Enychi questioned with a hint of irritation in her tone. "What you gon' do then? Huh... gamble your life away?"

"You crazy. Your man is too nice for that. I stay taking them dudes' money. Watch. You'll see.

"One day I'ma buy us a house, put about four carats on your finger and pay for one of them fairytale weddings—all for you—from the money I be winning from that shit, and then, I'll retire! Just wait. You'll see. Don't sleep on your man, babygirl!"

"Okay, Wa, w-h-a-t-e-v-e-r! "Enychi gave me a 'talk to the hand' gesture as she headed toward the bathroom. "I'll meet you around two—a 'ight?"

"A'ight, cool!" I said as I wolfed down my breakfast and headed out the door.

Pulling up on the block, I spotted Mel, Speedy and that nigga Dirty posted up in front of the corner store, looking like they was up all night. It was the first of the month so the fiends copped drugs until their money ran out. That was a good look for me, though, because I came to make money.

These dudes was some funny-ass muthafuckas. Mel was cool and known for getting paper. He had the block on lock with that crack shit. I use to run wit' him a couple of years ago, but I gave that hustle up after I caught that year-long bid.

He was serious about getting money so he didn't fuck around with that gambling shit too hard. When he did, though, it was all good 'cause he took his losses like a true player, but them niggas,

Speedy and Dirty, they ain't get them names for nothing. Speedy was quick to snatch up a few dollars when niggas wasn't paying attention, and Dirty - that nigga ain't never play fair. So with them two in the game, you had to watch 'em closely.

"Yo, what up, niggas?" I said, giving each nigga a pound. "What it look like?"

"Ain't shit, Wasuan," answered Speedy. "What up with you, kid?"

"Nothing. Ready to get this dice shit going. What's up? Ya'll niggas' pockets is ready—right ? 'Cause, yo, I'm ready."

"Hell, yeah, nigga," said Dirty. "These muthafucking pockets stay ready!"

"Yeah, nigga. Well, I hear you talking, but put ya money where ya mouth is!"

"Whatever, nigga." Dirty began counting out mad fives and ten dollar bills. "You ain't said nothing but a word. Bam! That's two hunnid right there—nigga, what!" Dirty threw the crumbled bills onto the pavement like they were on fire.

"Get the fuck out of here, nigga. I came to play. I ain't fucking around with no petty cash. But being that it's early and ya'll niggas wanna act like a bunch of broke asses, we could start shit off with five hunnid or better." I laughed, but I was dead up on some serious shit.

Mel threw his five one hundred dollar bills to the ground.

"Yo, count me in, dawg. I' ma go in the store and get some dice, 'cause word up, Wasuan. You been on some cocky bullshit ever since you won them last couple of games, but yo son, your luck's about to run out, word up."

"Never that, son," I confidently claimed as he went into the bodega. "Besides, luck ain't got shit to do with nothing—I'm just that dude that can't lose. That's all." Niggas got real tight as their pockets got lighter and mines grew fatter. The hours passed by quickly and more fellas came out to play. A lot of side bets jumped off, along with the arguments, 'cause in the hood niggas and money ain't a good mix and most can't ever accept their losses and let the shit go.

"Yo', come on, son," yelled cheating-ass Chico, another dude who thought his roll game was tight but always wanted a do-over 'cause of some bull-shit technicality.

"Run that shit back one more time. It hit my man's shoe!"

"Nah, nigga. Get the fuck outta here! That roll was straight, dawg. How many times you gon' run shit back? You aced out, you cheatin-ass mutha-fucka!" I picked up the dice and put them to that nigga's mouth. "Here blow on these, nigga," I joked as Chico cut his eyes at me and knocked my hand away.

"I'm about to kill it, a'ight...uhhhh," I said, tossing the dice to the pavement.

"Trips, muthafuckas. WHAT! Pick up ya face and pay-up. Damn, ya'll niggas ain't tired of me taking ya'll money yet?" I teased just get them niggas more agitated than they already was.

"I'm ready to play for real now. I got 10 Gs. What's up? Come on. Scared money don't make money!" I laughed as I challenged the crowd of about fifteen niggas standing around, but they ain't want it wit' me. Just as I was about to get into a bunch of shit-talking and name-calling on those scared, frontin'-ass niggas, I heard Enychi call my name.

"Excuse me," Enychi said as she fought to get past all the hawking-ass niggas admiring her fine ass. She was sporting a denim mini-skirt. "Hi. Can I get by?" Finally, she reached me. "Hey, baby," she said, kissing me softly on my lips before she continued. "You got that for me or what?"

I took her by the hand to walk her back toward her car and to get her out of the faces of them thirsty ass niggas.

"Yo, where's the rest of your skirt at? Didn't I tell you I was gon' have that for you? Here. Here's fifteen. Go buy you some fucking pants. I'll see you when I get home." I kissed her lips quickly and rushed her off .

"Okay, baby, thanks." Enychi had a smile on her face that could light up a room as she hopped back in her candy-apple red Dodge Viper and zipped off.

"Yo, how the fuck you pull her nigga—she bad!" Chico threw back his head and laughed.

"What, nigga! Yo, dude, stop sweating mines and put some real fucking money up so we can get a real dice game going!"

"Yo, word up, Wasuan." Tone rubbed his chin. "Shorty do look mad good! Is that wifey or one of them jump-off chicks?"

"Nigga, that's wifey, so wipe the muthafucking drool from ya mouth all ya'll thirsty-ass niggas and let's roll some fucking dice!"

"A'ight, cool." Tone nodded his head. "Ten Gs you said. That's it? Player, come on. That's what you call real money? I spend that shit on shopping for my chick's shoes, man!"

"A'ight then. Whatever, nigga! We could get right. How much you talking?"

"Oh, I know I could get right, but you sure you wanna fuck with me 'cause I know you ain't ballin' like that, dawg?"

"Yo, dawg. What, you tryna play me? You don't know how the fuck I'm rolling, so don't play me—play these muthafuckin' dice. Matter fact, call the bet."

"A'ight then. I'ma call it. Fifty grand off the top from me if you win and vice - versa if I win. Plus an extra ten until one of us roll trips."

I almost choked when Tone threw them kind of figures at me, but I wasn't gon' let him see me sweat 'cause I wasn't running from nothing. I came to win.

"Oh, you switching up the rules like that—cool!" I said in a skeptical tone.

"I ain't got that much on me now, but if I have to, which I doubt, I'll have my girl go in the stash and bring that to you."

"Yeah. Well, get ready to have her fine ass do that, nigga!" Tone responded sarcastically.

I was shitting bricks. I ain't gon' lie. My heart was pounding like a muthafucka as I shook them dice a little longer then usual before I tossed them to the ground like they were balls of fire inside my hand.

"Umm!" I shout as released the dice. I leaned close to see what I rolled. "Damn it!" I yelled again from disappointment. The dice read a 1, 6 and 7.

"Yeah, nigga. That's ten big ones to go with that fifty! You can handle sixty, right small time?" Tone threw back his head and laughed. Then he held out his palm. "Be ready to pay me mines, dawg. Word up, I got this. Bam!" He rolled, but it wasn't trips, either.

"Yeah, a'ight, yellow muthafucka! I'm 'bout to show you that light skin went out of style a long time ago. What we fucking with now—seventy? OK, OK, now that's what I'm talking about. Real money."

Tone rubbed his chin, but didn't say anything.

I kept on talking trash just to get under his skin, "You sure you ain't ready to quit now, you clown ass muthafucka? That's right, 'cause this right here is a grown man's game! I'm about to put a big dent in your pockets, dawg." I twisted my mouth to the side, then added for emphasis, "For real." I continued to talk shit 'cause that's what I do, but on the real, nobody ever had me under pressure like this. Then again, the stakes never been this high. Hell, I felt like I was going to see my P.O. with dirty urine on a day I knew she might ask for samples. That's how nervous this nigga had me.

I wanted to win so bad, my palms was sweaty and my dick was hard. I gotta win this, I kept telling myself.

"Come on, baby, come on," I pleaded as I kissed on the lucky dice around my neck before tossing the ones in my hand. "Please let these be trips."

I tossed the dice and looked to see what fell. "Shit! Still no good." I rolled a 2, 4 and a 5.

Tone stepped up to the plate. "A'igh, dawg. It's

over for you. I'm done playing with your punk ass. No more talk. Bam!!! Yeah, nigga. What! That's eighty big ones. Give it up!" Tone let out a whooping war cry as the crowd, roaring with excitement, started to jump around in celebration of his victory.

I just stood there shaking my head in disbelief as I looked down at the dice that read the numbers 6,6,6. Ain't this a bitch—the fucking sign of the devil.

Tone was hyped up and doing a lot of bragging and boasting , talking more shit than a little bit as he stepped to me and said, "Yo, you ain't call that pretty bitch of yours yet? Come on, dawg. Get on your horn. Call her up and tell to crack open your piggy bank."

"Yo, I see you got jokes. You got that, though. Just chill with all that, dawg. I'ma call her when I get ready to." I was trying to buy me a little more time to figure out how I was gon' break the news to this nigga 'cause I ain't have that kind of cash for this cat.

"What? Come on, dawg. You tryna play me now? I ain't waiting for mines. Bad enough I gotta wait for your broad to bring it to me." Tone started to sound a little hostile.

My hands continued to sweat like a muthafucka as the niggas that stood around started to clown the shit out of me saying stuff like, "You need a loan nigga?" and "Yeah, nigga. I thought you couldn't lose—where's all that loose shit talk at now, player!" I heard it all. Niggas was real reckless with the mouths, coming at me sideways with all their foul-ass comments. I had to think fast, though. I ain't wanna tell the nigga I ain't have it in front of everybody. I pretended I was dialing Eynchi, which gave me the opportunity to ease away from the crowd's noises. I was ready to make a run for it. No lie.

Only, that nigga Tone was definitely keeping his eye on me. "Yo, man, don't go too far," he said, watching me hard like a panther ready to pounce.

That nigga was really bugging the fuck out I thought, but he was serious about his paper so I ain't have no choice but to be a man about it and let the nigga know what the deal was. "Yo, let me holla at you for a minute," I said.

"Here we go with the bull shit," Tone said as he walked toward me.

"Check this out, yo. I only got half of the eighty right now, but I can have the other half in about a week or so."

Tone shook his head no. "Yo, dukes, is you trying to play me or something? Nah, dawg. I want all my cash, now."

"Well I ain't gon' be able to do it then. If I ain't got it, then how I'ma give it?"

"A'ight then, I guess it ain't nothing else to talk

about." Tone's voice remained calm as he pulled out his gun and pointed that shit in my face. Right then and there, the bitch came out of me. I started copping all kinds of pleas. Fuck it, I didn't care. My life was at stake.

"Come on, Pretty Tone, man. Why we gotta go there? I'ma pay you, dawg. My girl gon' bring you forty now and I'ma give you the rest by the end of the week, man. Just give me 'til Saturday - that's my word on everything I love. Come on dawg. Don't go out like that over no forty grand."

I started dialing Enychi for real this time 'cause dude wasn't playing. "Yo, 'Nychi. You home? Good! I need you to look in the drawer by the bed and get that key that's to my safe. Open it and bring me that money, a'ight? Hurry up!" I hung up before she could get the chance to question me. Besides I ain't have no time to be explaining nothing.

After I made the call, Tone put the gun back in his side. "Yo, if this was back in the days, you would of have been scattered all over this fucking side walk. I'ma work with you, though, but I need some type of collateral."

"Thanks, man. Anything. Yo, here take my chain, it's worth about ten Gs and the diamonds on this shit is official." As soon I took it off and finished the negotiating part, Eynchi was pulling up. Talk about a nigga feeling relieved and real happy to see her. That was me.

"Yo, man," Tone said. "Put your chain back on." Suddenly his eyes focused in on my girl. He continued, "I want something with greater value—I want your wifey."

"My girl?" My voice cracked. "Get the fuck outta here. What kind of shit is that?" This nigga was really trying play me like my name was Willie Lump-Lump. What the fuck was he on, some fucking indecent-proposal-type shit?

Tone pointed at Eynchi with his crooked finger. "Yeah, her right there. I just wanna fuck her. You could watch if you want, but I'ma put a hurting on that pretty ass, so you might not be able to handle that." He laughed.

"Come on, dawg. You real funny. How you wanna bang my girl out? Matter of fact, how I'ma tell her some shit like that? She ain't going for that."

Tone responded to my question in a cocky manner. "I don't really care how you tell her." He laughed like this shit was funny. "Fuck it. Tell her your life depends on it. I bet she'll go for that!" Tone was really trying to humiliate me to the fullest.

"Wait a minute. You for real?" I questioned for further understanding. "You saying, if I let you sleep with my girl, we even?"

"Nah, I'm saying, by me fucking your bitch—

that buys you more time to pay me the rest of my loot. That's all." Tone gave me a look that said, "Duh—you dumb muthafucka!"

I wasn't no bang-bang shoot-'em up kind of nigga, but I swear, I was ready to kill this muthafucka. I was at a hard point. Should I call this nigga's bluff or go along with this twisted shit? I thought about it. I really didn't have much of a choice 'cause I wasn't ready to die and my gut feeling told me not to chance it.

Feeling downhearted, I walked over to Eynchi's car, opened the passenger's side door and got in. I didn't know how the hell I was gon' ask my baby to do some bullshit like that.

"Wa, how much money is this? I mean this don't make no kind of sense—you need some help, boy!" Enychi went off on me instantly as she threw the plastic bag of money in my lap and sucked her teeth.

"You right, Ma," I agreed. "I do need some fucking help. I know this shit's crazy." I thought, I ain't never fucking around with them dice after this shit.

"All right, Wasuan. Get out my car now 'cause I know you gon' be out here all night, trying to win all that money back."

"Nah, wait a minute," I said, taking a deep breath 'cause I ain't even tell her the other half of it, and I could see Enychi was already fed up with my bullshit.

"I'm listening," she answered with a nasty attitude.

"A'ight. You was right when you said I need some help and I'ma get that, I promise. You do know that I love you to death, right, babygirl?"

"Yeah, I hear you." Enychi pursed her lips as she answered my question in a "whatevah, nigga" kind of tone.

She was making this so hard for me, but I had to continue. "Enychi, I need you to do something for me, not 'cause I want you to—'cause believe me I don't—but I need you to do it because you love me."

"Wasuan, what the fuck are you talking about?" she asked, slightly raising her voice.

"Just listen, a'ight? This shit ain't easy for me. I owe this nigga cash that I ain't got right now, so he's bugging the fuck out." As I continued, Enychi huffed and puffed, which was a surefire sign of her frustration.

I paused for a moment. This wasn't easy for me at all. "Baby, you see that light-skinned muthafucka standing over there?" With a discreet nod of the head, I pointed Tone out to her. Tone was staring back at both of us, a smug look written all over his face. Damn, I wanted to murder his ass right then and there for this. I took a deep breath, then blurted it out. "I need you to sleep with him for me or it's lights out—he's gon' murder my black ass."

"What? Wasuan, how much fucking money do you owe him?"

"All together eighty thousand," I mumbled. "This right here is only half of it."

Enychi sounded like a parrot as she repeated my words. "Eighty thousand dollars? Oh, you are so gone. Wasuan, I told you this fucking gambling shit was gon' get you in trouble. Now look at you. You gon' try to fuckin' pimp me to settle your fuckin' debt. Oh, hell no!" Enychi's arms were waving all over the car as her voice got louder. "What kind of shit is that to ask me? I'm not some fucking whore out in the street—I'm your fucking girl!" She frowned up her face as if she had just bitten down on a bitter lemon. "You a foul- ass nigga for even asking me some shit like that."

"Enychi, come on, Ma. You think I wanna have another muthafucka running up in you—my fuckin' baby? That's some bullshit, but you the one that jinxed me this morning wit' all the talk about me losin', and then you bring your mutha-fuckin' ass up here in some little short- ass skirt, talkin' 'bout 'excuse me', as you switched the fuck past that nigga!"

"Oh, so you tryna say it's my fault?" Enychi yelled.

"Nah, it ain't, and you right. I shouldn't even

have brought this shit to you. I fucked up so I'll deal with the consequences. Fuck it. Just let this nigga do what he gotta do and get it over with. As long as you know that I love you with all my heart and I always will, I'm cool going out knowing that." I hit her with the guilt trip as I started to make my exit from her vehicle.

"Wa—wait. You forgetting your money." Enychi's eyes began to water.

"Nah, I ain't forget it. You keep it. If this nigga gon' kill me regardless, I might as well die owing his ass the whole eighty grand, right?"

"No, wait a minute, Wasuan." Enychi reached out and placed her hand on my shoulder. "I'll do it. Go tell him I'll do it." She spoke in a pitiful, low-pitched tone that ate a nigga's heart up. I swear I felt like a straight sucker for going out like that.

Enychi's Side of the Story

I love Wasuan. I can't even front about it. He's everything to me. I always told him I would do anything for him, except rob, steal or kill, so I guess it was time to honor my word. But to sleep with another man over a dice game gone bad is crazy.

I couldn't understand how and why he would ask me to do something like that. I knew Wasuan loved me but I also knew he loved to gamble. Now I question which one he loved the most.

As he walked away, Wasuan beckoned for Tone to come over to my car. While Wasuan went back over to the crowd of men, probably to gamble some more, he didn't even look back at me. I was so pissed, I didn't care what happened to him.

Meanwhile, Tone walked over to my driver's side window. "What's up, beautiful?" he said as he held out his hand to introduce himself.

I gave a fake smile, but didn't extend my hand to meet his.

"You want my arm to fall off?" Tone said, talking some ol' Billy Dee Williams shit. I rolled my eyes at him hard 'cause I wasn't singing the blues and he damn sure was no Billy Dee.

"A'ight," he said as if he got offended by my look. "I know this is no doubt an awkward situation for you, but once you get to know me, you might fall in love."

Ahhhh, who did this Shamar Moore-looking, wanna-be-thug nigga wit' braids think he was?

Not only was he humiliating me and my punk-ass man, but the weak rap he was tryin' to run was tired. He seriously thought after one fuck, I'll fall in love. Nigga, please! I didn't even entertain his silliness. I cut my eyes at him again and asked, "So how you wanna do this?"

He laughed and said "Whoa, chill, Ma. Don't be like that. I'ma treat you like the lady you are— a little wining and dining first, a'ight? Just meet up with me tonight around ten, if that's cool?"

I let out a hard sigh and said yes, but to be honest, I ain't have the time to be spoon-feeding this nigga. If I had to fuck him, I wanted to do just that and be done with it. I guess he had other plans, though. He handed me his number on a business card that read "Big Tone's Urban Wear, Street Fashion for the thug in you" and told me to give him a call at about 9:30 so he could tell me where to meet him.

I studied the card before I stuck it in my purse. It was nice to see that he had a job, even better, his own business. That is, if the card wasn't fake, but he also had a certain style about him that had me a little curious. I agreed to the arrangements and pulled off.

I glanced around to see if I saw Wasuan, but I didn't. When I got home he wasn't there, either. I ran straight to the phone and tried calling him a few times, but my calls kept going straight to voicemail. It was six o'clock then. By the time eight rolled around, he still wasn't home nor was he answering my calls.

I had anger building up on top of anger. I couldn't believe he had the audacity to get us both in this mess, and now he couldn't even be man enough to come home and face his fuck up. My first thought was to not even go through with it, but then I thought how I would never forgive myself if something were to happen to Wa. I gave up on trying to contact him and headed for the shower.

After allowing the hot water to massage my body for about twenty minutes, I massaged it with some Moonlight Path body cream from Bath and Body and splashed on a few squirts of Be Delicious by DKNY. I'm a lingerie fanatic so it was nothing for me to go in my stash and pull out one of my brand new, black lace Simone Perele bra and panty ensembles. All the time, I was thinking, If this is going the be the talk of the town at least the nigga can't say I didn't look and smell damn good.

When I finished getting dressed, it was already a quarter past nine. I was so nervous, but I knew I had to go through with this. I tried my best not to put anymore thought into the situation at hand.

I grabbed my car keys, purse and Tone's business card and left the apartment. As I sat inside the car, Mario's "How could you?" played on the radio. I tried calling Wasuan one more time, but once again, my call went unanswered. I didn't bother to leave a message because the way I was feeling, I would have probably said something that I'd later regret.

I had no idea where I was meeting Tone, so before dialing him, I just sat in my car. First I had to get my head together and wrap my brain around what was going down. I took a deep breath. Time seemed to be moving extremely fast; the clock on the radio read 9:27. I took another deep breath, hoping that it would continue to move just as fast throughout the night as I pulled my cell phone from my bag and proceeded to dial Tone's number.

One the second ring, Tone picked up.

"A'ight. Punctual. I like that in a woman." Tone's voice sounded eager.

"Oh yeah," I said dryly. "Well, just remember. I'm not doing this 'cause I want to. So where do you want us to meet up at?"

"I'm not far from you so why don't I just come scoop you up?" Tone suggested.

"How do you know where I live?" My curiosity piqued.

"Come on, Ma. This is my 'hood. Ain't too much I don't know or can't find out. You in Rochdale, right? Circle One?"

"Yeah."

"A'ight, then. Come downstairs."

"I'm one step ahead of you," I said as I got out of my parked car and waited close the curb.

"That's what's up? I'm coming around now."

I heard a loud Vroom Vroom sound as I looked toward the entrance of my circle and spotted Tone - through a shiny black helmet - quickly approaching me on a Suzuki Hayabusa motorcycle. He slowed down in front of me and my thoughts escaped out of my mouth. "You can't be serious. I ain't getting on that thing."

Tone lifted his helmet, wearing a big grin on his pretty-boy face. "Ahhh, don't tell me you afraid?" he challenged me.

"Afraid? I'm not afraid! I just didn't know that's how you was rolling," I lied. Truth be told it turned me on to watch a man ride a bike, but I was scared as hell to partake in the ride.

"A'ight," Tone said. "Here's your helmet. Hop on then."

I hesitated. Finally, I fastened the helmet on, then straddled myself across the big black polished bike. I wrapped my arms tightly around his waist, squeezed my eyes shut and prepared for take off. The motorcycle roared when Tone revved the engine for the ride.

The wind blew mildly as we zipped in and out of traffic at a fast, but not intimidating, speed. To my surprise, it excited me. We reached the Greenwich Village section of Manhattan in fifteen minutes, and in three more, we were in front of this dimly lit Caribbean restaurant called Negrils.

I gazed around and nodded in approval. I had

to admit the restaurant's setting was a very romantic one. As the hostess seated us, a soulful mix of R&B jazz graced the air while the candlelight from each table flickered just the right amount of radiance off the walls. As we were seated, Tone stood up and waited until I was seated before he sat down. I was surprised but didn't let on that I was impressed.

Immediately after being seated, the waiter came over to our table and took our drink orders. Mine was a Chocolate Martini while Tone ordered a bottle of Pinot Grigio.

"Have you ever tried Pinot Grigio?" Tone asked.

"No, I'm not much of a wine drinker."

"Well, that's too bad because it goes pretty good with Caribbean food."

"This is a really nice spot," I commented.

"Yeah, it's cool. Is this your first time here?"

"Uh-huh."

"Well, I'm sure you've been to way more extravagant places than this."

I cracked a smile. I knew that was his way of indirectly trying to find out whether or not I had been out to nice places like this one before now.

The waiter came back with our drinks and took our food order. I ordered the Black bean soup for an appetizer, followed by the jerk shrimp, whereas Tone ordered a salad, oxtails and beans and rice. The restaurant was somewhat crowded and I could see why, 'cause not only did the food smell good, it tasted delicious. We continued the small talk throughout dinner as I constantly checked my cell phone and angrily wondered why Wasuan hadn't tried to call. The two glasses of wine on top of the Chocolate Martini had me feeling kind of buzzed and geared up to seal the deal, only, Tone wasn't ready just yet.

After he paid for dinner, he suggested we check out the restaurant's lounge on the lower level. Tone carefully held on to me as we walked down the steps. The art deco ambiance was just as chic as the upstairs, only the scene was a bit more intimate, and from the looks of it, the small crowd of people seemed to be enjoying themselves. Ironically, the DJ was spinning Maxwell's lyrics, "Maybe you might be more than just a one-night lady," from his Embrya CD.

We sat down in the only available spot next to the DJ and his turntables. As if on cue, the waitress rushed over and Tone ordered another bottle of wine. I was honestly enjoying myself, but, sadly, it made me realize what I was missing. Although I loved Wasuan, he never took the time to take me anywhere.

Most of his time was spent out in the streets gambling, and when he was around, his idea of showing me a good time was boning me until I was sore, giving me money and watching the latest DVD movies on bootleg together. What's funny is, up until tonight, I was cool with that. I couldn't miss what I never had.

When Tone told me he owned his own clothing store, as well as he had a degree in business management, I must say, his intelligent, hoodlum type of style intrigued me, and the fact that he was good looking made him even more impressive. We laughed at each other's jokes and even learned that we shared some of the same interests. I was trying my best not to like Tone, but couldn't help the fact that I already did. I never thought someone as thugged-out as he was could be the perfect gentleman. I guess that really goes to show, you should never judge a book by the cover. I even turned my cell phone off, thinking if Wa was going to call, or if he even cared, he would have done so by now.

"Damn, you're gorgeous," Tone said as he stared into my eyes.

I started blushing like a bashful little girl with butterflies in my belly.

"If you was mine, I would have just gave up the chain 'cause I wouldn't share you with nobody-" He paused in mid-sentence, took another look at me and continued. "Nah, I couldn't do that," he repeated as if he had just thought it over with himself.

I pondered over what Tone was saying. Was he

insinuating that Wasuan's lucky chain was an option and he chose to give me up instead? That can't be! Nothing in this world would have convinced me to believe that! He had just killed my mood with his lies, but I had to ask, "Were you really gonna kill him?"

Tone gave me a serious look.

"Kill 'im? Come on, now. Do I look like a killer to you?" He flashed a smiled at me. "Besides, I did a lot of time in jail for nonsense and I ain't tryna go back over no bullshit. But I will say this. I ain't no punk, though. A nigga ain't gon' just play me and get away with it."

"Well, look it's getting late. Let's not prolong tonight's intentions any longer." I was uptight all over again. I felt like I was seconds away from reneging on the deal.

"Damn, my bad, Ma. Maybe I shouldn't have took it there."

"Nah, don't worry about it. This ain't no date anyway; it's an arrangement, right? So let's just get out of here, go do what we gotta do and get it over with." I couldn't help but take a cheap shot at him in return for the one he took at me, especially since his remark had me questioning whether or not it was really a cheap shot or the truth.

"Yeah, I guess you're right," Tone said as he signaled the waitress to close out his tab.

With no hesitation, I hopped on the back of his bike. As he zoomed through the city's streets, I couldn't help but bury my head into his back and tightly clutch on to his waist. I could smell his cologne. He was wearing 212 by Carolina Herrera, which was one of my favorite men's fragrances. I knew that scent from anywhere. I purchased it for Wasuan, but he never wore it, so I sprayed our bed sheets with it instead.

Tone not only smelled good, his body felt just as good. He was all muscle, like he worked out and took care of himself, which was another thing Wasuan neglected to do. Even though Wasuan was tall and skinny, he still needed to get in somebody's gym just to get fit. I realized that not only did this guy have me paying closer attention to him, but he also had me doing a lot of comparing.

What is that about? I had to check myself because Wasaun was still my man, and no matter how mad I was at him, I loved him and I was doing this for him and only him. Tone pulled up to the Wyndham hotel near the LaGuardia airport.

"Wait here," he said as he got off the bike and walked through the hotel's revolving doors. Minutes later, he emerged with a smile. He reported that the room was on the first floor located on the outside. We found an open parking spot directly in front of the room door.

As soon as we entered the room, we got straight down to business. With eager strokes, Tone started to firmly caress my body. As he softly kissed me with conviction, I found his tongue game to be so intoxicating that I couldn't help but anticipate the feel of him French kissing my pussy. Instantly, I soaked the seat of my panties, wondering if it was the alcohol making his touch feel so good to me or was he just that fucking good? But as he gently bit down on the nipples of my breast, chills shot through my body like shock waves, and right then and there, I knew he had skills.

Stopping abruptly, Tone got up off of me and demanded, "Take off your clothes. I'll be right back." He then grabbed the empty bucket from the dresser, went out of the room and returned in minutes with a bucket full of ice cubes. I quickly undressed and lay on the bed. My naked body quivered impatiently, awaiting his return.

Mesmerized by my nudeness, he swiftly removed his clothes as I checked out every inch of his body, and I swear to God, LL's six pack couldn't fuck with his, even after the plastic surgery.

Damn, Tone was fine. I almost climaxed from the sight of him. His dick wasn't yet fully erect, but I could tell Wasuan had him beat in that department because he was hung like a horse even when he wasn't hard.

Tone walked over to the bed and kneeled down.

Slowly separating my legs, he began to insert the ice inside of me. My hot box liquefied each cube instantaneously. As the water trickled down my pussy, he started to finger fuck me amazingly, before finally diving in face first. I grabbed hold of his braids and hungrily fucked his face with my hips as he slightly lifted me from the bed and licked me from my ass to my clit until the walls of my coochie started to throb.

Closing my eyes, I welcomed this never-felt-before high that came over me. The utmost feeling of ecstasy had taken its place and my entire body began to jerk. I released multiple orgasms in one of the most intense climaxes I'd ever felt.

"Ahhhhhh," I moaned. My whole body shuddered as tears seeped from the corners of my eyes. Dumbfounded by the feeling, I didn't utter a word. Tone finally came up for air, wearing my juices all over his face. From his smile, I could tell he was just getting started as he hopped up from the bed in an overconfident manner.

Walking toward the full-length window, Tone slid back the curtains and placed the chair in front of it. "Sexy, c'mere," he called.

I eased myself off the bed to go to him. At first my knees buckled, I was so weak.

"Hold on to the top of the chair and bend over for me," he whispered as he palmed my hips. I let out a soft sigh when he slid his hardness inside my wet pussy. Instructing my body to follow his lead, he slowly worked my middle. Fucking me from behind in front of the window got both of us excited as a couple walked by and stared.

To tell the truth, Tone's sex wasn't as good as his foreplay, but I found myself putting on a show for our viewers and I started to become a little more aroused. I grimaced in contorted facial expressions and let out loud obscenities. Obviously, Tone was turned on by my over-exaggerated performance so much that he started to aggressively dig up in my guts like a wild animal and talk real raunchy.

"Tell me you're Daddy's little whore," he said, smacking me on my ass.

He threw me off with that kind of talk. I didn't know how to respond so I didn't answer at all.

Pop, pop, pop. Tone spanked my ass three more times, causing it to sting as he demanded, "Let me hear you say it!"

"Yes, I'm Daddy's little whore," I yelled out in a pitch that said satisfaction.

"Damn...work it, bitch, work it! Yeah, just like that—don't stop. Do that shit, Ma! I'm 'bout to come. Ahhhh—yeah, right there—right there!" Tone stuck his finger in my mouth and I bit down on it as he unload a full load of nut inside of me, and then shut the curtains.

Together we both flopped to the bed, fulfilled

and exhausted. We fell fast asleep.

When I woke up the sun was rising. I eased out of bed, put on my clothes in a hurry and left. As I stood in out front of the hotel lobby and waited on a taxi, I turned on my cell phone on to see if I had any messages. To my surprise I had twenty-five. The first five were from a very apologetic Wasuan, expressing how much he loved me and how he felt like less of a man for putting me through this.

Fifteen voicemails later, he was all over the place, placing all the blame on me, saying things like we set him up, it was over between us, I must have wanted it, how could I let a another nigga fuck me, and how, if I really loved him, I would of been answering his calls.

This boy has really gone bananas, I told myself. I wasn't gonna trip 'cause for one, Wasaun wasn't a drinker, but from the way his words slurred, I could tell he was drunk. Two, there was no doubt about it, although I might have enjoyed last night, I did it for him, and it's over with.

My cab pulled up and as I opened the door and sat in the back seat, I could feel Tone's come oozing out of me. Damn, I played myself. I got so caught up in the moment that I didn't even ask him to use a condom. I wasn't worried about getting pregnant because I was wearing the patch, but thoughts of contracting a sexually transmitted disease scared the shit out of me. How could I have been so stupid? The last thing I needed was for Wasaun to find out I let Tone run up in me raw.

It was a little too late to start thinking smart, but just to be on the safe side, I knew I was gonna have to hold off on sexing Wa for a few days.

As soon as I opened the door to our apartment, I spotted Wasaun passed out on the couch with two empty pint-sized bottles of Hennessy lying down on the floor next to him.

My first instinct was to go over to him and slap the shit out his face, but for what? I just had the best sex of my life. Not only was it six in the morning, but the situation felt so awkward that facing him was something I didn't look forward to, so I wasn't gonna wake him. I eased past him and went straight for the shower.

Wasaun asked me to do it so I knew I didn't have any reason to feel guilty, but I did because I'd liked it. I scrubbed the sweat from my body and douched Tone's come from my pussy, wondering if my relationship would ever be the same. Still feeling drained, I fell in the bed and went straight to sleep.

Later that morning, when I woke up, Wasaun was already gone.

Wasaun's Side of the Story

I couldn't help but wonder if Enychi had a good time last night, especially since she brought in daylight and tried to sneak past me this morning. Damn. All I kept thinking about is how that nigga fucked my girl and still expected me to pay his ass the rest of the money. That alone should have broke us even. I had to make moves, but knew I was gon' be the comedy for the day on my block so I headed way on the other side of town to get my money up.

My game was way off, but I managed to win a bullshit five hundred to go with the five I had from the few broke niggas that was out. Around my way, I knew dudes was good for at least three or four grand in a few short hours, but I had to get my head right before I could fuck with them niggas. I hit up my man Jamaican Jack for a fat dime bag of what he called that yard weed, got me a Dutch and sparked up a nice blunt. Now I was game.

As soon as I hit the block, I saw the little dudes posted up on each corner on the look out for the boys in blue, so I knew the fellas had to have a serious game of dice already popping. When I walked up, niggas started laughing out loud and shit. But I kept face; my mind was on getting money. I was high, my confidence was strong, and I ain't have shit else to lose.

Without even asking what the bank was, I said, "Yo, I got the ends on what's left in it."

That's when these foul-ass dudes really tried to come at me crazy. I was hearing it all. The nigga Dirty was singing, "If that's your girlfriend, she wasn't last night."

Chico's hating ass was holding the bank so he was on some, "Yo, the bank is a thousand strong. If you lose, nigga, I got next, a'ight? Not on the roll. I'm talking 'bout wit' that fine ass broad of yours!"

He didn't know it yet, but he had it coming to him for his comment, but I disregarded all of the disrespect long enough to get my count up. My anger was motivation. I hit c-low on my first roll which brought my pockets up to 2 G's.

"Yo, fuck you, nigga," Chico yelled. "Stop the bank!"

"Whatever, dawg. My bank is two thousand. Ya'll niggas know the rules. Trips pay double." I prepared for my next roll. I threw the dice and landed a 6,7, and 8, which would have meant I aced out, but since one die was leaning from a crack in the pavement and couldn't be stacked, I got to run that back. I caught trips, quadrupled my dough and walked away with the bank 'cause niggas ain't wanna fuck with the game or me no more.

Before I broke out, I walked over to Chico and

punched him in his punk-ass mouth. I was tight about that slick shit he'd said earlier, and I had to gain some respect from somebody so why not start wit' that nigga.

"Have next on that, BITCH!" I walked to my car, grilling every one of them niggas, waiting for one of them to say something. I got in my ride and sped off. I was thirty-four grand away from getting out of Tone's debt, but there had to be another way 'cause I was gonna start making enemies real fast if dudes kept up the disrespect.

When I walked in the crib, Enychi was in the living room on the couch getting her laugh on as she watched "Strange Love" on VH1.

"Hey, how you?" I spoke nonchalantly as I walk past her to the bedroom. All of a sudden I was feeling strange about our love. Now don't get me wrong. I loved her and I knew she fucked Tone because I asked her to, but part of me wished she would have stood her ground and told me to kiss her ass.

"Baby, can we talk?" Enychi asked as she now stood at the door of the bedroom.

"What? Right now?"

"Yeah, right now. What's up with you? Why do I feel like you're avoiding me? I called you a million times last night and you couldn't call me back once?"

"I did call you back," I answered in an irritated

tone.

"Yeah, after the fact. But I'm talking about before I even left the house."

From her approach, I could tell that Eynchi was just as annoyed with me as I was with her.

"So did that nigga fuck you good last night, since it seems like you took one look at that pretty muthafucka and had a change of heart about sleeping with him?"

"Hold up! Are you trying to say that I wanted Tone? Oh my God, I don't believe you. This was your fuck up. You're the one that put the price tag on my body. You fucking ingrate."

"Ooooh, ingrate," I said sarcastically. "Huh. Well, it's good to know that all the money I'm kicking out for your education ain't going to waste."

Enychi's facial expression turned bitter. If there's one thing she hated, it was having something that I done for her thrown up in her face. I knew I'd hurt her with that comment and although those were my intentions, I felt bad after I said it.

"Damn, baby, I'm sorry. It ain't you. It's me. I feel like less than a man for letting that shit go down—that's all. I'm ready to kill that nigga."

"Wasuan, can we just forget about him and this whole situation? Let's just go back to it being about you and me, baby." Eynchi walked over to me and wrapped her arms around me tight. "I love you and only you, Wasaun Jameek Wells," she said, addressing me by my full name.

"I love you, too Enychi Michelle Carter." I did the same, kissing her lips passionately as I started to undress her, curious to see if the pussy still felt the same to me. I wanted her badly. Enychi was gonna be my wife one day so no matter how many the negative thoughts entered my mind, I still kept trying to convince myself that she did it for me.

Eynchi's Side of the Story

I felt nervous. I really didn't wanna have sex with Wasaun, but after the argument we just had I knew he was feeling insecure. Telling him no would only make matters worse. I went along with his sexual advances. So as he kissed me, I kissed him back.

Wasaun's Side of the Story

I secretly inspected Enychi for marks as I worked my lips from her neck to her pussy. As I buried my face in her pus and gently rotated my tongue through her nappy dug-out, my dick went limp.

I lifted my head. "Did you make that nigga wear a condom?" I questioned

"Wa, come on. What kind of question is that?"

"It's the kind that better get answered 'cause you smelling funny down there!"

"What? Just get off of me. You're fucking tripping"

"Oh, I'm tripping? Well, you still ain't answer the fucking question." I wasn't gonna let up until she did.

"And I'm not gonna answer that question—go ask Tone if he wore a condom, you asshole! That's it. I'm out of here." Enychi got up and started putting on her clothes.

"Oh so you want me to ask him? Where you going?" I jumped up and grabbed her by her wrist. Take off your clothes and let's lay down. I'm sorry!"

"Wasuan, why are you doing this to me? Enychi started to cry as she continued pleading. "There's no reason to feel insecure. It meant nothing to me. Baby, it was just sex, OK? You asked me to do it so I did it and that's it. Now, please, let it go!"

"OK, OK, I will. But, did you suck his dick?" I knew I was pushing it.

Enychi cut her eyes at me and didn't say a word.

"A'ight, a'ight. I'm letting it go!"

* * *

As the days slowly passed, my situation with Enychi had gotten worse. When I wasn't losing my erection, I was drilling her with questions like; was he better than me, bigger than me or whether or not she enjoyed it? I never felt so much regret before now.

Trying hard to get this money up had me stressing the fuck out. I had three days to hustle up twenty-two thousand and niggas wasn't betting enough cash to help me get it. I had to put that dice shit to the side, and for a minute I jumped back in the drug game. I partnered back up with my man Mel so I could try and flip my dough. I got me a pre-paid cell phone and made deliveries to the high-end fiends. Selling crack really wasn't my thing. They say stick to what you know and since I wasn't tryna go back to jail, I stayed low-key.

Tone would zoom back and forth through the block on his bike just to add more pressure. He saw me going hard. Although dudes had chilled out with all the jokes and the gossip was finally dying down on the streets, I felt like Tone was trying to rub the situation in my face 'cause he ain't never rolled through the block like that before. We locked eyes a few times. Tone wore this smirk on his face that said "Yeah nigga, I fucked your bitch, and no, I don't respect you."

The thought of murdering that dude crossed my mind many times, but body bagging a nigga just wasn't in my heart.

I took my frustrations out on my girl more and more. No matter how hard I tried to let it go, my insecurities still managed to move full speed ahead. I questioned Enychi's whereabouts and watched her like a hawk when I could. I turned into a jealous lunatic, all up in her shit. I didn't trust her. I'd check her cell phone, her purse and even her panties, just to see what they smelled like. And, yeah, I still loved her, but our relationship had become so distant. I didn't know how to fix it.

Eynchi's Side of the Story

Wasuan was driving me up a fucking wall. Ever since I slept with Tone, our sexual endeavors have been replaced by limp-dick disaster. It's like, he's not even attracted to me anymore. And since a girl has needs, I found myself creeping around with Tone every chance I got. It wasn't easy with Wasaun keeping tabs on me the way he does, but when you really want something, it's not hard to get around the obstacles that stand in the way. My heart was still with Wasuan, but sexing Tone was adventurous, spontaneous and fulfilling.

Besides, after seeing how stressed out Wasaun had been lately, I thought if I continued to fuck Tone, maybe I could get him to squash the forty thousand as a favor to me. I wanted to save my relationship with Wasuan, but his jealousy was pushing me away from him. He still spent a lot of his time out on the corner doing what he does, but he called my cell phone every thirty minutes. On occasion, I was bent over in a doggy-style position, getting pounded–out, but Tone would slow it down and hit it quietly until I got off the phone. It seemed like the only time I could get away for a few hours without Wasuan calling constantly was during the hours I had class. So instead of doing class, I would make plans to do Tone.

Wasuan's Side of the Story

I waited for Eynchi to park her car and enter the building before pulling off. As I reached the second traffic light heading away from her school, I noticed a Suzuki bike that looked just like that nigga Tone's heading in the direction I just left.

Hold the fuck up. I made a U-turn and parked my car crossways from Enychi's school. Watching her face light up at the sight of Tone as she kissed his lips the way she used to kiss mine had me vexed. I couldn't believe this bitch was skipping out of classes that I was paying for to creep around with that muthafucka. She threw on his spare helmet, hopped her ass on the back of his bike and they took off like they was down with the Ruff Riders.

I kept my distance as I followed them to a Brooklyn movie theater. It was 11 a.m. Who fucks with a movie at that time of morning? I thought.

Immediately after they purchased their tickets, I entered the empty theater. I saw them go into auditorium #9; "The Grudge".

I bought my ticket and fucked around with the video games for about fifteen minutes or so until the previews played out.

When I walked inside the movie, it was dark, but it didn't take long for me to spot them out because they were the only two in there. Enychi wouldn't have noticed me or anyone else because she was already too busy on her knees. Tone's head was leaned back and his eyes were closed. He looked like he was in fucking bliss, so it wasn't hard to figure out what was going on. Especially since I knew what it felt like to have my dick in her mouth, too. I got on some sneaky shit myself as I dipped down low in the aisle until I found the best seat in the house - directly behind them. I watched my chick bounce up and down on this nigga's dick like she was a professional fucking bull rider. My blood boiled, and tears came to my eyes, but I let them rock.

Staring at the two of them only angered me more as all the coulda, woulda, shouldas invaded my brain. I only had myself to blame.

Instead of telling that nigga to suck my dick, I welcomed him to my girl. I knew I didn't handle Tone like a real man was supposed to, so I couldn't even be mad at him for snatching her up.

It's real when they say what makes you laugh can also make you cry 'cause Eynchi brought joy to my life. I loved her. Now I'm crying and fucked up on the inside while that nigga's getting his laugh on. I couldn't let it go down like that. I got up and left the theater, still unnoticed. My hand was forced and revenge was gonna be as sweet for me as the joy of fucking Eynchi used to be!

ORDER FORM

Triple Crown Publications
2959 Stelzer Rd.
Columbus, Oh 43219

Name: _____

Address: _____

City/State: _____

Zip: _____

	TITLES	PRICES
	Dime Piece	$15.00
	Gangsta	$15.00
	Let That Be The Reason	$15.00
	A Hustler's Wife	$15.00
	The Game	$15.00
	Black	$15.00
	Dollar Bill	$15.00
	A Project Chick	$15.00
	Road Dawgz	$15.00
	Blinded	$15.00
	Diva	$15.00
	Sheisty	$15.00
	Grimey	$15.00
	Me & My Boyfriend	$15.00
	Larceny	$15.00
	Rage Times Fury	$15.00
	A Hood Legend	$15.00
	Flipside of The Game	$15.00
	Menage's Way	$15.00

SHIPPING/HANDLING (Via U.S. Media Mail)   **$3.95**

TOTAL $_____

FORMS OF ACCEPTED PAYMENTS:

Postage Stamps, Institutional Checks & Money Orders, all mail in orders take 5-7
Business days to be delivered.

ORDER FORM

Triple Crown Publications
2959 Stelzer Rd.
Columbus, Oh 43219

Name: _____

Address: _____

City/State: _____

Zip: _____

		TITLES	PRICES
		Still Sheisty	$15.00
		Chyna Black	$15.00
		Game Over	$15.00
		Cash Money	$15.00
		Crack Head	$15.00
		For the Strength of You	$15.00
		Down Chick	$15.00
		Dirty South	$15.00
		Cream	$15.00
		Hood Winked	$15.00
		Bitch	$15.00
		Stacy	$15.00
		Life Without Hope	$15.00

SHIPPING/HANDLING (Via U.S. Media Mail)   **$3.95**

TOTAL $_____

FORMS OF ACCEPTED PAYMENTS:

Postage Stamps, Institutional Checks & Money Orders, all mail in orders take 5-7 Business days to be delivered.